SENSUAL SACRIFICE

Ilene could not believe this was happening to her. First, the brutal abduction. Then the drug she was forced to swallow, injecting into her body an uncontrollable hunger for a fulfillment she shuddered to imagine. And now the figures who entered the room, surrounding her as she sat tied in a chair, clad only in a black diaphanous gown.

She saw men and women, wearing loose cloaks over their nakedness and hideous masks over their faces, whirling drunkenly, lewdly, in a frenzied dance. Then they parted to make a path, straight toward her, for a huge creature seemingly half-man, half-goat.

"I have chosen you especially," his voice boomed out. "You are about to be honored by me. Do you understand?"

And as she felt his hands upon her, Ilene understood all too well . . .

. . . and there was no one but Satan and his slaves to hear her screams. . . .

#14
KATHERYN KIMBROUGH'S
Saga of the Phenwick Women
ILENE,
THE SUPERSTITIOUS

POPULAR LIBRARY • NEW YORK

POPULAR LIBRARY EDITION
February, 1977

Copyright © 1977 by John M. Kimbro

ISBN: 0-445-03181-6

Dedicated to Thelma Tharp

PROLOGUE

Patricia had grown old in the flesh. No one was more aware of that than she. The mind was still young. The spirit would always be one wonderfully free and able to express itself wherever it may be. Even though the body was tired, the least bit of challenge was a stimulant to her and she rallied back again and again.

She had willed herself for years to remain young. But there is a time when even the most avid spirit tires of the physical stress it must endure and longs, as if magnetically drawn, to escape the mortal agony it has been forced to experience.

Still the learning process will continue, as it is doing for me. I've learned things that one in the physical could never possibly begin to comprehend. And how many levels of awareness are there even in the body expression?

Perhaps life is easiest for the superstitious, who believe in a kind of world of fantasy. Sometimes it is distorted illusion, an impossible faith in an improbable hypothesis. Still they cling to a promised hope of a never-never land. Others encounter different levels of existence in the physical as if they are able to break through some vibrational

5

facade: some into the spirit world, others into various levels of earthly beings.

Legend has kept man alive for centuries. Even the most sane individual enters a realm of fantasy every now and again, and dares to believe such legends. While I never experienced any such awareness when I was living—and would Augusta Phenwick ever have allowed herself such folly?—I had heard of myths and folklore passed from generation to generation.

But I did not investigate such things, so I learn of them over here—wherever *here* is. Although I become a little bored with the wait, I never cease to marvel at the things I learn—much more than I was willing to open my mind to as the dominant head of the Phenwick family. Now I watch and learn from the experiences of the others.

CHAPTER ONE

1856

Dr. Joseph Ornby was a huskily built man with a large frame. While still in his twenties, his brownish blond hair had begun to thin, giving him a high forehead. His round face had good features and a ruddy complexion. He made an impressive if not altogether handsome appearance. Devoted to his work, the young physician followed as eldest son of Dr. Theodore Ornby in his profession, as did his next younger brother, Augustus. Dr. Ted, as Theodore was affectionately known to his patients, was proud of his first son when he completed medical school with top honors. Even more he was delighted that the youth wished to continue further in the study of the mind in the infant field of psychology.

Dr. Ted had a cottage on Tremont Street which he converted for his office facilities. The building was large enough that both of his sons could set up practice in it if they were so inclined.

Augustus was still in Europe studying, and Joseph had plans to return in the fall for another year of education in Vienna. One day he hoped to found a school of psychology in Boston or Cambridge that other less affluent Americans could learn of this vast field to be explored. Both of the Ornby lads were excellent students who during those years took little time for a personal life, believing they wished to be well established in their professions before they selected wives.

Joseph worked on charity cases when not tending to his small following of private patients. "You've got to give to others if you want to receive," he would always say. By then the needy of Boston were an ever-increasing horde, especially with all of the immigrants who had invaded the city. Since the late 1840s, countless numbers of starved Irish had migrated across the ocean. They lived in shanty squalor, most of them, which was a breeding ground for disease and contagion.

One afternoon Joseph entered his father's office after the last patient had been seen. The large youth wore a perplexed expression.

"What is it, Son?" the father asked.

"There has been an epidemic of deaths throughout this winter among the immigrants. The Irish settlement has been particularly hard hit."

"Boston wasn't prepared for such an onslaught of foreigners," Dr. Ted returned. "They're not our responsibility."

"They are," Joseph argued, "if a serious epidemic erupts from them. It could jeopardize the lives of everyone in the city, rich and poor alike. I've made several case studies in the past few weeks. For example, I have been visiting the Dumphy family—talk about gross poverty—and attending to ailing Mrs. Dumphy, who has wasted away to practically a skeleton with sickly skin covering it. I've made every test I know of, and can only reach one conclusion."

"What is that, Joseph?"

"Malnutrition What else can it be? That's the story among those people," Joseph continued. "Mary Dumphy has existed solely on a meager portion of cabbage and potatoes all winter. Sean Dumphy, the husband, has had no work. He keeps hoping that he can find something by spring. The two older boys are out on their own and supply as much to the family as they can. The eldest child, a daughter, looks after the younger children. There's ten living children."

"Living?"

"Mrs. Dumphy lost three children at birth in the last five years" Joseph commented.

"That would also explain her weakened condition," Dr. Ted observed, leaning back in his chair and tapping his fingertips together in front of his beard. "With two boys away, that would still leave eight children at home."

"No. Fortunately, Molly, the second daughter, has obtained a position as a domestic," Joseph said, "which gives her room and board and little else. She's being exploited."

"Still there are seven."

"The next daughter is going on eighteen," Joseph went on. "She, too would like to find work as a domestic. The five younger children, with the exception of the next boy, are far too small to work. Chauncy, who is number six, is old enough to work—perhaps in industry. But there just aren't positions for boys when men are unemployed." He had a distant look. "Sheila, the eldest, is obliged to take care of the children. A pity, too."

Dr. Ted studied his son. A dim smile. "Sheila? I take it this Sheila is a rather attractive young lady?"

9

"Oh yes, extremely," Joseph answered almost too quickly. "I mean she's pretty enough. All of the daughters are attractive, comely lasses."

"You'll forgive my observation, Son," Dr. Ted said with a brief chuckle, "but I'm beginning to perceive why you have such an interest in this— was it Dumphy family?"

"Yes, the Dumphys."

"And you believe that as long as the last of the children is to be looked after, lovely Sheila will not have a chance to live a life of her own. Isn't that the case?"

"It's quite true, Father, but—"

"Yes, but. But it would be nice if she weren't so obligated, wouldn't it?"

"That was what I was thinking."

"I thought as much. Well well, Joseph. I'm glad to hear you're having such thoughts," Dr. Ted commented. "It's time you were. In the old days, I would contact Aunt Patricia about such matters. It was she who arranged for me to meet your mother."

"Arranged? I'm not looking for any kind of arrangement." Joseph protested.

"Aunt Patricia arranged for me to meet Louise at a very sociable gathering," Ted continued. "Aunt Patricia used to handle such things quite well. Neither of us had an inkling what the old lady was up to. I won't say it was love at first sight. But by the time I saw your mother for the third time, there was no doubt in my mind about her. As we both know, your mother's side of the family is in an excellent position socially and financially."

"Socially and financially?" Joseph bit contemptuously. "Is that all that is important?"

"When you come from wealth, as we do, Joseph." Dr. Ted said, measuring his words, "it is advisable to perpetuate it by marrying into more wealth."

"I never expected to hear you speak this way, Father."

"I'm sorry if I must be brutally frank," Dr. Ted returned. "Aunt Patricia has always said it was best to look among your own kind. That way you don't leave yourself open to disaster."

"I don't believe what I'm hearing."

"I'm sorry if I have disillusioned you, Son. I have great compassion for people—all people—and a deep love for my children, you especially as the eldest. Cliché as it may sound, you are my pride and joy. And Augustus comes second—but that is his chronological place. I put great faith in you two—I put faith in all of my children. That I've always maintained."

There was a knock at the outside door.

"It must be an emergency of some kind," Dr. Ted responded. "All of my regular patients know it is after my usual office hours."

"I'll go, Father." Joseph hurriedly left the room using the exertion to release part of the anger that had risen in him. "Miss Dumphy!"

The pretty dark-haired young lady with cold blue eyes stood staring at the man. Her eyes were red from crying. "Would ye be allowin' me to cum in?"

"By all means. It's cold out there. Come into my father's office, he has a fire going," Joseph stated, taking her by the arm and leading her to the inner room. "This is my father, Dr. Ornby. And this is Miss Dumphy."

"Pleased to meet you, Miss Dumphy," Dr. Ted said. "Miss Sheila Dumphy?"

"Aye, that is me name," the young woman replied. "I've cum simply to tell you that you need no longer cum look in on me mither. She's gone."

"Dead?"

"Aye. At ten past three this afternoon," Sheila replied. "She wanted a priest, but none would cum because she belonged to no parish."

"No priest?"

"Me mither was a Catholic, all right," Sheila said, barely controlling tears. "Me father, while a descendant o' Orangemen, was unchurched, as is th' case with me brothers and sisters and meself. She all but gave up religious belief, I thought, until it came to th' last hours. Sure'n she was scared. Me father said it was from old red-neck superstition. Himself went out a-lookin' for a priest for her. I would have cum sooner, but I had to care for her. 'Tis sad, I am beyond words." She broke into tears.

Impulsively Joseph caught her in his arms in an understanding embrace. He held her comfortingly for several minutes. Ted observed. It was an act of compassion he would have done for any person in a time of grief; it was natural that his son should respond in such a way. Still he noticed more in his son's attitude as he held the weeping woman.

"You shouldn't have come out in all this cold, Miss Dumphy," Joseph soothed. "You should have sent one of your younger brothers."

"They are as grief-stricken as meself," Sheila returned, managing to control her sobs. "Me mither was a brave woman. She has had her a hard life with little comfort. 'Twas her blessin' and me own curse I was born th' oldest. She could have never handled all that brood by herself and havin' children one after the another. Then to lose th' last three—which I do say was a blessin' in disguise— was very hard on her. She tried her best to give us learnin'. We all can read and write. Me father can only make an X for his name. She could never learn him."

"You're an intelligent girl, Miss Dumphy," Joseph commented, still holding her. "You should learn easily."

"Most o' me brothers and sisters have good sense," Sheila said. "Jamie is a bit dense, but he's still young and full o' play. What's to becum o' him now? Aye, what's to becum o' all o' us? 'Twill nay be a pleasant wake. But th' neighbors have brought in a thing or two."

"I will drive you home in the shay," Joseph volunteered.

"That is nay necessary, Dr. Ornby," Shelia replied. "I can make me way with no problem. I need to walk to help th' grief pass."

"May I come and call to pay my last respects this evening?" Joseph asked.

"If you like, sir," Sheila nodded to Ted. "Pleased to have met you, Dr. Ornby. I'll be goin' now."

"I'll see you to the door."

Dr. Ted was standing with his backside to the fireplace when Joseph returned to the cozily warm office. He watched his son's confused movements. "So that was Sheila Dumphy, was it?"

"Yes." Joseph sat heavily in a chair. "I might have been able to save that woman, if only—"

"If only she hadn't been a breed sow and had had better food."

"That's being unkind, father."

"But truthful," Ted grunted. "If we had known

13

she was on her way out, we might have sent Gordon to call on her. Although he is so radical, he's liable to have scared her. Still he could have prayed for her, and she might have taken some peace in that."

"It's too late to think of what we might have done," Joseph said. "Mr. Dumphy will be next. He's not a strong man. The whole family is an example of gross malnutrition."

"Sheila looked fairly healthy to me."

"She is healthy now, but she has youth on her side," Joseph commented. "I spoke with several physicians in London when last I was there, all of whom were convinced that nutrition is an essential ingredient to a person's well-being. Another ten years of nothing but cabbage and potatoes will make Sheila look like an old woman. I have great pity for her—and her family."

"Understandable." Dr. Ted stepped to where his son was seated and placed a hand on the strong young shoulder. "My son, if you are to be a successful doctor, you must learn to detach yourself from your patients."

"You mean become callous and unconcerned?"

"Not unconcerned, Son," Ted stated. "There's a difference. You must always have concern for their problems, the conditions you are treating, but to become personally involved—well, that could place you in a very strange position, and it could be very taxing to your own emotions. Certainly reach out with compassion to assist as best you can without becoming involved."

"I see what you mean," Joseph sighed, "but that is something they did not teach me at medical school."

"Even with Aunt Patricia, our own relative,"

Dr. Ted continued, "it is necessary to maintain a detached attitude if we are to adequately diagnose her needs."

"Aunt Patricia? The rich old lady on the hill," Joseph bit. "She won't die in squalor. Far from it. She will go in opulent luxury as she has lived." He turned to his father. "Will you go with me this evening?"

"Go? To Edward House? I was planning to."

"No. After we go to Edward House and see dear Aunt Patricia," Joseph said, "I would like you to go with me to the Dumphy's."

"If you wish, I would be pleased to, Joseph. We'll go home and have supper with your mother, then ride to see the bereaved."

"You may not be able to hold your supper down, Father, once you see the way the Dumphys live," Joseph returned, rising to get his greatcoat. "Let us go to notorious Edward House then and get Aunt Patricia over with."

CHAPTER TWO

Joseph and his father were greeted at the door of Edward House by Dietrich, the butler, who spoke with a heavy Teutonic accent. Moments later they were met by beautiful Marcia Phenwick, who welcomed them each with a kiss. Always radiant, the young lady was a joy to behold. Joseph had long envied his Cousin Stuart for having such a gracious wife.

"Two handsome doctors at once," Marcia stated. "Grandma*ma* will be pleased. Even in her weakened condition she still likes company."

"We're not company."

"Not in the usual sense of the word," Marcia returned lightly. "But she always looks forward to your visits."

"We'll go right up."

"Stuart should be here by the time you've finished with her," Marcia said. "I know he will want to have a word with you. And, Dr. Ted, I think you'd better plan on examining me in the near future."

"Are you not well, Marcia?" the older man asked.

She laughed. "I'm not concerned about an illness, just a condition that married women often find themselves in."

"Ah! We'll take a few minutes once I'm finished with Aunt Patricia."

Patricia Phenwick had grown feeble over the winter months. Traces of youth that had lingered long in her face had vanished. She looked old and withered. Still her mind seemed to be as sharp as ever. She obviously experienced much pain.

"Ah, Teddy, there you are," Patricia exclaimed as best she could, but her old greeting was distorted. "It is good to see you again, Joseph."

"My son is going to examine you, if you don't mind, Aunt Patricia," Dr. Ted said.

"Breaking him in on the route, are you?" Patricia questioned, her voice cracking and husky. "Oh yes, I recall you're planning to go abroad again this spring. I don't say I envy you. I always found those long crossings tedious and fatiguing. I was not destined to be a sailor, as you well know."

Joseph took the old woman's pulse count. "Have you been experiencing any pain, Aunt Patricia?"

"Constantly."

"Where?"

"All over. It even hurts to fold my hands," Patricia stated. "Ah, they were once such lovely hands. I received so many compliments. But most of those who were so generous with their praise are no longer with us. That goes to prove what a relic I've become."

Joseph listened to her heart and examined her tongue and eyes.

"If you're looking for a breeding mare, you've come to the wrong stable," Patricia commented. "With my two granddaughters married, I'll surely be verging on great-grandmotherhood. I detested

17

the thought of being a grandmother; you can guess what a promotion of that sort will do to my morale. Well, the legendary Patricia Phenwick is just that—a legend. I wonder if the outside world realizes I'm still alive—furthermore I doubt if anyone cares."

"You still have your fine sense of humor," Ted commented.

"If you think that was funny, Teddy, this handsome young doctor is examining the wrong one of us," Patricia returned. "I'm glad you permitted Joseph to give me a going-over. It's nice to know the touch of youthful male hands again." Suddenly she burst into a fit of coughing. "Oh God! If I'm not expiring, *why* not?"

Joseph patted her hand sympathetically. "Aunt Patricia, you're in good shape for a woman your age."

"That well may be," Patricia said as she gasped to recover from the coughing, "but how many people live to be my age?"

Joseph chuckled. He motioned to his father that he wanted to leave. "I'll call on you again tomorrow, Aunt Patricia. In the meantime I suggest you stay as much in bed as possible."

"More time in bed? At best I sit up for four hours during the entire day," Patricia replied. "I found the winter scenery dull, but I am looking forward to watching my garden as spring comes."

Both men kissed the old woman patronizingly on the cheek before they left. Patricia sat propped up in bed. Anger came over her. She could not stand being confined. Her life had been too active for that. Wouldn't it be better for her to dance and live as actively as possible, rather than to sit and deteriorate in bed? But she could not dance anymore. She could not even leave her room on the second floor, much less navigate going down the stairs.

"What do you think, Joseph?" Ted asked as they got outside in the hallway and out of earshot of the door to Patricia's room.

"Her pulse is low, her heart is weak," Joseph said. "There's a terrible raspy sound in her chest. Illness in her eyes. Frankly, she's slowly decaying, and there's nothing we can do about it. I'm of the opinion, if Marcia is indeed pregnant, that Aunt Patricia should have around-the-clock attention. Hire girls to come sit with her, to take care of her needs, to be companions. What little it would cost would not even make a ripple in her vast wealth."

"Do you feel she is as bad as all that?" Ted questioned.

"Father, she is in danger of hurting herself. A coughing attack like she had could take her before help could arrive," Joseph said. "And if she tries to get out of bed by herself much longer, she's liable to fall and hurt herself. Someone needs to be at hand to assist her. If she were to break a bone, her misery would be compounded. It's the only sensible suggestion I can make."

"Then we'll approach Marcia and Stuart about the matter," the older man remarked. He went to the head of the stairs.

"The first remembrance I have of Aunt Patricia when I was a small boy, was when she was standing on this identical spot. Wide billowy skirts on all sides of her, diamonds and other precious stones sprinkled about her, and she made the grandest entrance down these steps that I have ever seen. I had never seen anything so elegant in my life. My father informed me that she was his wonderful Aunt Patricia. I can still see her to this day. What we left in that room back there isn't the same person. It's sad."

Joseph put his hand to his father's shoulder. "And you're no longer in knee breeches, Father— nor am I or any of your children. Still we all learn to adjust with time. Shall we go down? Marcia will be waiting in the parlor."

Even Dr. Ted's step was slower as he took the stairs. He tried to pass it off as the result of his being absorbed in thought, but Joseph knew otherwise.

Marcia had prepared coffee for the doctors in the parlor. She did not rise when they entered.

"Stuart has not returned home yet," she stated. "He'll be along shortly."

The men sat to have coffee.

"How is Grandma*ma*?" Marcia inquired.

"Old," Joseph returned. "The parts are tired."

"Joseph suggests she needs constant attention, Marcia," Ted commented. "It is his idea that you should hire a couple of girls to come and sit with her, one for the night hours, one for days. There are enough girls looking for work; surely you could get them for next to nothing and they would be delighted to have the work. Besides, if you are in the condition you suspect you might be in, then you cannot and should not have to devote too much time with her."

"I think it a very good idea," Marcia returned. "I confess I feel the confinement of being with her so much of the time. True, she spends several hours a day telling me about the Phenwick family, then I go and write it down. Later I take it back and read it to her. Sometimes it's only a few pages, no more than five or six. She says it's a combination of our creative talents."

"It will be good to have a family record, even as seen through the eyes of Aunt Patricia," Ted remarked.

"And the eyes of Marcia Phenwick. Don't discount that, Cousin Ted," Marcia said lightly. "May I pour you coffee?"

Dashingly handsome Stuart Phenwick arrived. Being informed by Dietrich of the whereabouts of his wife, he went instantly to the parlor. Greetings were exchanged, small talk indulged in.

After Stuart agreed wholeheartedly to the notion of having girls come to sit with Patricia, he asked if he might be excused to go freshen up a bit.

"Joe, if you don't mind, I'd like to have a brief chat with you while I change," Stuart commented.

Joseph, while comfortable, was glad to have the opportunity to speak with his cousin.

"What is on your mind, Stuart?" asked Joseph as they reached Stuart's dressing room.

"It's my brother."

"Gordon? What's he up to? Saving all of Boston with his evangelical ravings?" questioned Joseph.

"He's trying to," Stuart laughed. "But that is nothing new. He has a mission, says he, and he's determined. So far he is disappointed in me. Yet I think he conceded that battle as lost a long time ago. What frightens me is Gordon's extreme fanaticism. I thought my mother was bad, but he's twenty times worse, and worsening with every passing day. It frightens me."

"Why should it scare you?" asked Joseph, propping himself against a table. "Specify."

"I let him have his game of playing evangelist," Stuart returned. "That isn't the problem. It's what it's doing to him. Inside. On one hand I see the old Gordon, on the other I witness a kind of monster emerging. It's as if he has to compensate for his ultra-good side by being just the opposite."

"I still don't understand what you're getting at," Joseph stated.

"He's like a coin with two sides. He's a nest of contradictions," Stuart said, trying to laugh lightly at it. "I can't put my finger on precise incidents nor can I tell you why I have these suspicions. It's a feeling I have. I know my brother—probably as well as anyone can know him—and I'm convinced all is not right with him. That is all I can tell you. The changes I have seen are so subtle they can slip past and only on second thought do they strike me as being different—unusual."

"That's all very speculative, Stuart," returned Joseph, altering his position only slightly. "Have you spoken with any of his associates?"

"No. They're about as erratic as he is. There's a certain kind of person who goes in for his way of thinking," Stuart observed.

"Why should you become concerned about this?" Joseph asked.

"Because he is my brother."

"Are you afraid his behavior will reflect back on you?"

"It well could."

"But there is something else disturbing you about the situation isn't there?" Joseph continued. "I would judge it stems back to your mother, her ways and her disastrous death."

"That has entered my mind."

"At the end," Joseph suggested, "you did not believe she was herself, to put it in a nice way, did you?"

"I confess I didn't. Or at least I didn't want to," Stuart replied. "When I think back over that entire situation, I am convinced something had happened to her. She actually hired a person to practice voodoo on Nancy and another to carry out the threatening details. Still she proclaimed that voodoo or any of the occult was the work of the devil."

"You don't think Gordon is—?"

"Nothing so bizarre," Stuart returned. "He mentions her often after all this time, throwing her up to me as a reason why I should change my ways. Find salvation, as he calls it."

"Do you feel that you need to find such?"

"No. I like the way I am. I'm loving and happy. I can't see how I could possibly want more out of life than I have at this moment."

"A son perhaps, if Marcia's suspicions are correct," Joseph said. "Or a daughter. But do you in any way feel a sense of guilt about your mother's death? You were there at the time."

"Grandfather convinced me there was no way I could have saved her from that burning house," Stuart said. "At the time, admittedly, if he hadn't held me back, I would have run into the house and probably been consumed by flames myself. Yet, if my mother had lived through that ordeal, there was enough evidence against her to have— well, I shudder to think what might have happened to her."

"What do you want me to do about all of this?" Joseph asked.

"I don't know. Maybe just to be aware of it,"

Stuart said. "If circumstances change, I may need to come to you for advice."

"You're not responsible for Gordon's actions."

"But if I can help him in any way—"

"Ah yes. I will make a point of going to see your brother. Maybe we can have a rational chat. We've never been close. Frankly, I've steered clear of him and his eccentric ways."

"I will appreciate anything you can do, Joe. Even if you just observe him. I might be the one with distorted vision."

"I doubt that, Stuart."

A short while later Ted and Joseph Ornby were riding in the carriage toward the run-down area of town where the poor people lived in miserable hovels. Both were silent for a short while.

"Aunt Patricia has agreed to hire two girls," Ted reported, "but only two. I suggested that three would lighten the burden for all of them, but she was determined in her decision. I thought I would have a more difficult time than that in convincing her."

"There was a young woman who tended Mrs. Ashcroft in her last days," Joseph mentioned. "Stella Murphy is her name."

"Another Irish girl."

"The poor Irish people need work, Father," Joseph argued. "And they'll work for less than anyone else just for the opportunity. Stella was a good worker and was always reliable. She prefers, however, to work at night. We'll need to find a girl for the days."

"What about your Miss Dumphy?"

"Sheila?"

"She seems able-bodied."

"She is," Joseph returned. "Why do you call her *my* Miss Murphy?"

"I meant to say your friend. The way you comforted her this afternoon would indicate you had some kind of friendship with her," Dr. Ted said.

"Only that of a patient and doctor," Joseph commented, becoming a little flushed. "Actually we simply met because of her mother."

"I see." Dr. Ted stroked his graying beard.

"Sheila—that is, Miss Dumphy—has her hands full taking care of that family," Joseph added. "There are at least two small children under ten— and the father. He's not well."

"Perhaps one of the other Dumphy girls."

"I don't know who is after Molly—and Molly is employed by a wealthy household," Joseph commented.

"It's only a thought," Ted murmured as he gave his attention to the passing movement on the street. "You're a braver man than I am, Joseph, coming down into this neighborhood alone."

"I go where I am needed."

CHAPTER THREE

The neighbors had been as kind as they possibly could be. They brought what food and drink they could spare for the bereaved family. It was the least they could do when Mary Dumphy had been as good to them as she had been. A more affluent Irishman, who owned a tavern, furnished beer. By the time the doctors arrived at the abomination that passed as a house, Sean Dumphy was well into his cups and feeling no pain. Both Tim and Paddy had drunk their share, and even Sheila had had a few to perk up her spirits.

The younger children were teary-eyed and confused. Chauncy, the sixth child, opened the door to the men. He had had one cup of beer and it had made him sick. The red-eyed boy, who was about sixteen, recognized Dr. Joseph Ornby. He motioned them into the largest of the three rooms, where the body was laid out on the table.

"Some o' th' neighbors are makin' a coffin for her," Chauncy explained. "Won't be ready until later tonight."

Sheila presented herself to the doctors, offering them each a cup of beer. They declined. "Mrs. O'Leary baked some sweets if you would care for one."

"No, thank you," Joseph said. "We just came to

pay our respects and to examine the—your mother."

"There's no hidin' her, there she is," Sheila commented, pointing. "We're just waitin'. Th' place isn't big enough for a proper wake, but it's th' best what we've got."

As the doctors viewed the body, looking for any evidence of contagion or disease, a low keening came from the dark corner of the room. Joseph turned to see who was causing the noise.

"Pay no attention to her, Dr. Ornby," Sheila said. "That's just me sister. She's superstitious and carries on at wakes and th' like. It's just her way. You can stop that for a while. Do you hear me, girl? 'Tis you I'm speakin' to, Ilene!"

The plaintive, whining noise in the corner softened, but continued its mournful dirge.

Attractive Molly Dumphy arrived while the doctors were examining. She had just been allowed to leave her place of work. Immediately she went into convulsive sobs and threw herself crying on her mother's body.

Ted nudged his son and motioned for them to leave. Joseph put his hand to Molly's shoulder, but his touch was little comfort at that moment. He patted gently and left with his father, saying a quick goodbye to Sheila, who had gone to tend to Molly.

Joseph was about to pull the carriage door closed after giving instructions to the driver, when he was interrupted by a soft voice calling his name. Believing it to be Sheila, he crawled out of the vehicle.

The sweet, pretty face looked up at him. A black shawl coverd her hair. In that faint lantern light the color of her eyes was not discernible. "I was wantin' to thank you for cumin', Doctor."

"My sympathies go to you and all your family," Joseph said. "I was only too happy to come. I can tell you're not Sheila. And Molly couldn't have overcome her weeping so quickly."

"I am Ilene, I am," she said in a gentle, falsetto-like whisper. "I'm just behind Molly. I was fond o' me mither, but, bein' in th' middle, I was nothin' special to her. But she did teach me to read and write. And I was th' one who sat at her feet and listened to all th' stories she had to tell. 'Tis true what me sister said, I am superstitious. Th' night before last I heard the banshee wailin'. Yesterday I saw an ugly ol' woman a-washin' clothes in th' stream—washin' blood from them, she was. It was th' signs that death was cumin'. I know."

"Do you believe in that sort of thing, Miss Ilene?" Joseph asked.

"Oh yes, Dr. Ornby. Once you've heard the wail o' th' banshee, you never forget it," Ilene said with conviction. "'Tis a terrible moanin' sound that cums in th' night. I was awakened from me sleep. 'Tis fearful, it is, and makes th' wee hairs stand up all o'er you. Me mither—I am almost certain she heard it, too. We sleep three and four to a bed, but I was able to wiggle me way out. There, standin' at th' window, I saw me mither. She had a faraway look in her face. I knew th' banshee was wailin' for her. And I believe she knew it, too."

"You do?"

"Aye, she seemed to sigh with relief, it was that pronounced, it was," Ilene continued. "I know o' th' long and terrible suff'rin' with what she's been plagued. She niver let on much to any o' us, but I could tell. Then Moorduke confirmed me suspicions."

"Moorduke?"

Ilene hesitated as if she had not meant to say that. " 'Tis a friend o' mine. He told me for certain it was a banshee what was cryin' in th' night, and that it was me mither's time. But he said I should nay fret, but rejoice for her. I confess a tear o' loneliness has cum to me eye, but nay one o' sorrow. Me mither is at peace at long last."

"Does this Murdock live close by?"

"He lives near enough. And his name is Moorduke, not Murdock," Ilene corrected.

"Miss Ilene, my father is waiting for me in the carriage," Joseph explained. "There's a chill in the night. And pity the poor driver."

"Aye, 'tis wrong to keep you any longer. I only wanted to thank you for cumin', that is all. Besides I must git back to th' wake. Moorduke will be displeased."

"Was this Moorduke in the house?"

"Aye, he is with me most places. He's very small and inconspicuous to most eyes. Goodnight, then." She waved, turned and went into the house.

Joseph stood a moment scratching his head before he returned to the carriage.

"What was that all about?" Dr. Ted inquired, anxious for his son to close the door.

Joseph tapped on the top of the carriage, a sign to the driver. The vehicle lurched forward. "A very strange girl. I've not seen her before on my visits to the Dumphy's."

"What about her?"

"Have you ever heard the expression 'banshee,' Father?"

"Sounds like a tribe of Indians somewhere," the older man commented. "No, can't say that I have."

"And while we were in the house, did you happen to notice a small male person?"

"I noticed the young lad they called Jamie," Ted replied. "I would say he was close to ten, but small for his age."

"No. She said he was small and inconspicuous," Joseph muttered as if he were speaking to himself.

"I would say she has a remarkable vocabulary for a person of such poor means," Ted said.

"Yes, I noticed that. She speaks with a marked accent, yet her brogue was not as thick as Sheila's or any of the others'."

"You find her fascinating, don't you, Son?"

"Only because she was so unusual. I felt as if she didn't quite belong to that family. Don't ask me why, I can't explain that at all. I only know I had a kind of strange reaction when I was speaking to her." Joseph sat in silence mulling over the conversation he had had with Ilene Dumphy. Then he sighed deeply and turned his mind to other thoughts.

Two days later Joseph approached his father after going over several papers on which he had been working. Dr. Ted's last patient had left for the day.

"May I take a minute of your time, Father?"

"What is it?" Ted stretched and felt fatigued.

"I spoke with Stella Murphy today."

"Stella Murphy?"

"The young lady who sat with Mrs. Ashcroft in her final days," Joseph refreshed his father's memory. "She is most anxious for another position. I took her to be interviewed by Aunt Patricia, and the old girl accepted her right off. That's a bit of luck. The only thing Aunt Patricia said to me later was that she thought Stella was quite common and not much of a conversationalist because she didn't appear to have much of an imagination. But Stella is moving in tomorrow. I hope dear Aunt Patricia is as easy to please with the second girl."

"The second? Have you found one?"

"No. But Aunt Patricia's mention of Stella's lack of imagination caused me to think."

"Aunt Patricia has always been eccentric," Ted commented, "for as long as I've known her. She likes unusual people around her. As much as I dearly love and admire Marcia, I could never stand to have her around me for lengthy periods of time. She is too animated for my tastes. But she suits Aunt Patricia fine. Why, over the years, I have encountered such a singular train of people coming and going to Edward House—all of them close friends of Aunt Patricia—that at times I wondered about her. She likes the artistic, the imaginative, the bizarre. Being a writer herself in earlier years, that kind of creative person seems to challenge her thoughts and her moods."

Joseph chuckled to himself. "You are finished early today. It's still daylight outdoors by an hour or more."

"So it is. Some days are like that."

"If you don't mind, I won't go home with you, Father," Joseph said as if he had had a sudden turn of thought. "I've a patient or two to call on yet."

"Go on, Joseph," Ted said. "I'll putter around here for a while longer, then trudge home. It's a good walk and I can use the exercise after a long winter without it."

The more he considered the idea, the more he was convinced that it was sheer inspiration. No doubt Patricia Phenwick had given up the struggle because life no longer presented a challenge to her. If such a challenge were presented, she might just very well rally new strength. Joseph did not know that much about her character. Marcia had informed him that the final stages of the Phenwick history were being written. There would be rewriting and editing, but the basic work was near completion. The old lady needed a new project to occupy her mind.

A short while later the shay, which Joseph drove himself, pulled up in front of the shanty occupied by the Dumphy family. Young gawky Mickey Dumphy was approaching the house from around behind it. He was hitting the siding with a stick.

"You! Young Dumphy," Joseph called. "Is your sister Ilene at home?"

"Aye, I'll fetch her," the boy returned, running into the house.

A few moments later Mickey appeared in the doorway and Ilene pushed past him.

"Did you wish to see me? Oh, 'tis you, Dr. Ornby," Ilene said.

"I would like to have a few words with you. Shall we take a short ride?" he asked.

"Me mither told me niver to take rides with strangers," she said lightly. "But me mither's no longer here—and you're hardly a stranger."

"Is your friend Moorduke around?"

"Aye, he's about, I have no doubt," Ilene replied, reaching her hand for Joseph to give her a hoist.

"I should like to meet him."

"That would nay be possible," Ilene returned. "He does nay appear much to strangers—nay much to anyone, me own brothers and sisters included."

"He sounds a bit elusive," Joseph commented as he bounced the reins. He called back to the boy in the doorway. "Tell your sister Sheila that I'll bring Ilene back within the hour."

"Where are we goin', Dr. Ornby?"

"Are you frightened?"

"Nay, ye do be a good man, I can tell."

"What does Moorduke think of me?" asked Joseph.

"He hasn't expressed any thoughts one way or t' other," Ilene replied. There was laughter in her voice.

"What's your age, Ilene?"

"Goin' on eighteen. I'll be a fair woman ere long."

"I was thinking as much," Joseph remarked. "That is, as a doctor I have noticed that you have developed into womanhood. Still there is an aura of the little girl around you."

"You're a fine large man yourself, Dr. Ornby," Ilene said. "I have noticed."

Joseph laughed loudly. "I hope I haven't given you the wrong impression, Ilene. I have come to interview you for a position."

"A position?"

"Would you like to have a job? A live-in situation."

"Aye, that I would like next to more than anything in th' world," she stated.

"Next to?"

"Aye, me first choice would be to have a man, I'll nay mince words with you, Dr. Ornby," Ilene said, a hint of a plea in her voice. " 'Tis too many mouths to feed in th' Dumphy house. You, bein' a doctor, can check me over. You'll see that I'm strong and healthy. I have all me teeth and me body is full and round."

Again Joseph laughed. "You are a fair prize for any man, I should say. But before you get carried away with your attributes, I want you to know I'm not seeking a wife for myself."

"I have me principles," Ilene said, "but they can be stretched a bit."

"No, no Ilene. The position I wish to discuss with you is in the employ of an elderly woman. My aunt." Joseph flipped the reins.

"With an old lady?" Ilene sounded disappointed.

"Do you know where Beacon Hill is?"

"Aye, I've sauntered up there a time or two, and had dogs sicced on me," she explained. "One old man came out shakin' a cane and hollerin' he didn't want any shanty Irish up around his house. I was mindin' me own business, too. I believe Moorduke must have done somethin' to th' dogs 'cause they turned tail and went a-runnin'.' "

"Moorduke again? Was Moorduke with you?"

"He's usually somewhere nearby. He's gotten me out o' a fix or two."

"What kind of fixes have you been in?"

Ilene laughed brightly. "Oh, I've had mē moments. Don't get the wrong impression o' me, Dr. Ornby. I try to be a very good garl, but sometimes I chance into situations what can be difficult."

"Tell me more about Moorduke," Joseph persuaded.

"You're not even from th' old country," Ilene commented. "I don't think you would understand about th' likes o' Moorduke."

"What sort of man is he?"

"Well, he's not precisely a man."

"A boy then?"

Ilene hesitated. "I have to ask you a question first, Dr. Ornby. Do you believe in fairies?"

"Fairies?"

"Aye, the wee people," she said uneasily.

"I've heard legends about them," Joseph said, trying not to sound alarmed. "Is Moorduke a—?"

"I might as well tell you," Ilene replied softly. "You may not want me for th' position with th' old lady when I tell you. Moorduke is a leprechaun."

"A leprechaun? One of the little green men of Irish folklore?" asked Joseph not certain he had heard correctly.

"He's a little man, but he's nay green."

"And he is your leprechaun?"

"No. I am *his* person. For some reason he has adopted me as his very own," Ilene explained in all sincerity. "It isn't often a leprechaun chooses to accept a person o' his very own."

Playing along with the story, Joseph asked, "I thought leprechauns only lived in Ireland."

"They do—most o' them. But not Moorduke. I was only six years old when he found me one day in th' forest," Ilene explained. "I had fallen to sleep in th' woods, that tired I was. What I didn't realize was that I was lyin' right in th' center o' a fairy ring. When I woke up, there was Moorduke. He was furious because I had knocked over one o'

35

his mushrooms. Once he got over his rage, he told me to pay for th' damage I had done that I was to become his human. Me mither told me that it was queer he would want me since persons usually want to find a leprechaun to locate his crock o' gold. But me mither knew that I had seen the fairies from th' time I was a wee breath o' a lass. She came one day and found them playin' on me bed when I was sleepin'. You can't ask her now, but she would have told you it was true. She said I was an exceptional child and th' fairies were a sign to her." She laughed. "You don't believe any o' this, do you?"

"The question is, do you?"

"When Moorduke is as plain as th' thumb on me hand, wouldn't you believe?"

"I suppose I would." Silent for a minute, he suddenly laughed. "Aunt Patricia is going to love your sense of humor. She likes an active imagination."

"Moorduke isn't only in me imagination, Dr. Ornby. To me he is very real."

"Of that I have no doubt, Ilene. I didn't mean to laugh at you," he said gently. "I think you are wonderful. One further question and we'll return to your home. Is Moorduke with us now?"

Ilene turned about. "Aye, he's there in back, sittin' on the edge, danglin' his feet. 'Tisn't often we get to go for a ride." She called back. "What do you think, Moorduke, about me workin' for an old lady? He says 'tis th' direction he's been pushin' me in. Whatever that means."

Joseph laughed loudly and encouraged the horse to a fast gallop. There was no further conversation until they reached the miserable shanty.

"I'll be here to pick you up at eight in the

morning, Ilene Dumphy," Joseph stated. "Will you be ready?"

"Aye, that I will." She jumped down from the carriage. "Thank you for a lovely ride. 'Twas enjoyable. I'll be ready, Dr. Ornby."

"Goodnight, Ilene." Joseph waited until the girl got into the house and turned back to wave again before he motioned for the horse to go forward.

A short distance down the road, the doctor stopped the carriage, hopped down and went around to examine the back of it. He half expected to see a leprechaun still sitting there.

CHAPTER FOUR

"Those were her exact words, Father," Joseph said the next morning. "I confess she almost had me believing in the little man."

"Irish superstition," Ted snorted. "I've heard tales from some of the patients. They believe in the little people. It's a means of escape into a world of fantasy."

"All peoples have their legends," Joseph commented. "When I was at Harvard, there was a professor who had done a vast amount of research about folk legends. He was of the opinion that many of our modern-day religious beliefs are based on legend and superstition. That was only his thought, I hasten to add, and it was expressed to me in private. I sometimes wonder if some of the distortions of the mind aren't caused by irrational superstitions and blind convictions."

"That's a peculiar statement, Joseph."

"I haven't time to explain it now, Father. I promised I would pick Ilene up at eight o'clock. Besides I want to organize my thoughts better on the matter before I try to explain myself."

"You will stop by to see me this afternoon, won't you, Son?"

"Yes. Now I've got to get Ilene up to be interviewed by Aunt Patricia or my entire day will be gone before I know it," Joseph said as he dashed from the room.

Ted gazed after his son and chuckled with amusement.

"What do you have wrapped in that bundle, Ilene?" Joseph asked as he reached her place a short while later to find the girl waiting, a straw bonnet on her head and two shawls about her shoulders.

"It's all me earthly belongin's," she replied, tossing the bundle into the back of the shay. "I've nay got much. When I told Sheila you were going to take me to see about a position, she said I was to get me things together and be prepared." She climbed up onto th seat beside the man. " 'Tis good to see you today, Dr. Ornby. 'Tis going to be a fine day, I can tell. I feel it in me bones."

"And what is Moorduke's opinion?"

"He agrees with me." She laughed.

Dietrich was alarmed to see Dr. Ornby present himself at the front door with the likes of Ilene Dumphy. Although he was first-generation European, the butler looked down on other foreigners. Still he knew that Joseph Ornby was a Phenwick somewhere back along the line. The man tried not to sneer as he appraised the pretty but nearly ragged-looking girl.

Ilene gawked. She had never seen a house as spacious or as elegant as Edward House. The foyer and entrance hall alone were about the size of the entire Dumphy home. She whistled.

"We'll go upstairs," Joseph said after giving the butler instructions to announce him to Patricia Phenwick.

"I feel out o' place in this fancy place, I do,"

Ilene exclaimed. "Me dress is clean, but 'tis hardly what a person should wear in a palace like this."

"This isn't a palace, Ilene," Joseph explained as they climbed the stairs. "I will admit it is a mansion of considerable size. As to your attire, I have no doubt you will be supplied with other clothes more suitable to your position."

"If th' old lady likes me."

"The old lady's name is Mrs. Phenwick. Can you remember that?"

"Aye, I have a very good memory. Wasn't I ready when you cum to pick me up?" Ilene questioned impudently "Me mither always said me mind was as sharp as a whip. Even Moorduke, he says—"

"And that's another thing, Ilene," Joseph warned, stopping at the head of the stairs. "If I were you I wouldn't mention anything about Moorduke on this first interview. Aunt Patricia might not understand."

"Oh, I usually keep Moorduke to meself. Leprechauns bein' as uncommon as they are in Boston, 'tis best, I've found," Ilene commented with a sober expression.

Marcia came sailing out of her room across the hall from the one belonging to Patricia Phenwick. The pretty young lady seemed to glide in her long skirt as she approached her cousin and the girl. "Well well, have you brought a second girl today, Joseph?"

"A second?" Ilene questioned. "D' you mean there is someone else?"

"Two girls are needed, Ilene. Have no fear," Joseph assured her. "Ilene, I would like you to meet Mrs. Phenwick."

"You said she was an old lady," Ilene blurted out.

Marcia was amused. "There is more than one Mrs. Phenwick, Ilene. I am one of the young Mrs. Phenwicks. Grandma*ma* is the one who will interview you."

"Oh. 'Tis pleasant to know th' doctor here knows young from old," Ilene commented impudently.

"I assure you I know the difference quite well, Ilene."

Marcia was grinning broadly as Dietrich appeared at the door to Patricia's room and held it for the guests to enter. Joseph had to prod Ilene to hasten her along. He placed a hand at the center of her back as he guided her toward the chair in which the elderly lady was seated. Ilene curtsied.

"Come nearer, child. I won't eat you," Patricia commanded. "A pretty thing, aren't you? What is your name, girl?"

"Ilene. Ilene Dumphy," the lass said timidly.

"Irish no doubt. With a name like Dumphy, what else?" Patricia remarked. "I understand you've recently lost your mother."

"Oh, she's nay lost. We know quite well where she is," Ilene returned. "I tapped the soil down with me own foot, I did."

Marcia giggled.

"As to her spirit, I do believe it's hoverin' about somewheres still to watch o'er us. She was that way," Ilene explained.

Patricia attempted to chuckle, but her amusement developed into a spell of coughing.

"Here now," Ilene volunteered, "let me give you a rap on th' back. 'Tis th' best thing when wind

41

has got down th' wrong pipe." She went to the chair and Patricia allowed her to pat her gently on the back. "Me brother Jamie once swallowed a fish bone and we all pounded and pounded on him. It came up. You were askin' about me mither."

"It's unimportant," Patricia commented as she regained her composure. "Have you ever sat with an old lady like myself before?"

"Nay. I have done a bit o' scrubbin' in some o' th' big buildin's in th' city," Ilene related. "Me brother Tim got me th' work. I got blisters on me hands and calluses on me knees, I did. But Moorduke—that is, a friend told me I was nay destined for that kind o' work."

"And what type of work did this friend believe you were destined for?" Patricia questioned, gaining interest in the remarkable girl.

"Well, Moorduke—" She cast a glance at Joseph, who frowned. "That is, me friend has queer notions at times. To me I am his princess."

Patricia cocked her head with amusement. "His fairy princess, no doubt."

"Nay, nay that." She laughed as the thought tickled her. "He knows better than that. And well he should."

"I don't quite follow," Patricia said.

Joseph stepped forward. "Ilene has a very active imagination, Aunt Patricia. And once you get her started talking, it's difficult to stop her. I think you should stay with conversation pertinent to the position."

"Why don't you want the girl to talk, Joseph?" the old woman curiously inquired.

Joseph shrugged and stepped back, rolling his eyes as he turned toward Marcia.

"I take it this young man is your gentleman friend," Patricia mentioned.

"Well, nay in so many words, he isn't."

"I'll not ask you to explain that," Patricia continued. "Your personal life is basically your own business. As long as it doesn't interfere with your job. I will offer you lodging and food along with a few dollars a week. If I find you're worth it, I'll give you more. If I find you're not, I'll dismiss you. Is that clear?"

"Perfectly clear."

"You sound educated, Ilene. Are you?"

"Nay, missus, only what me mither learned me."

"Taught you," Patricia corrected.

"Aye, that is what I said." Ilene caught herself. "Oh, you mean I used th' wrong word. Taught. I must remember that."

"She's bright, Joseph," Patricia commented. "And just impudent enough to be interesting. You say she has an imagination?"

"Quite an imagination, Aunt Patricia "Joseph assured her.

"Good. That other one is dull as clabber," Patricia said. "I'd rather have a bright girl sit with me during the daytime. You have no objections to living in?"

" 'Twould be a pleasure, missus."

"It's Mrs. Phenwick, if you please."

"Aye, Missus." Ilene beamed. "Phenwick."

"How soon can you start?"

"I've brought me things."

"If what you're wearing is an example of your other things," Patricia muttered, "you will be needing a few new clothes. I don't think I could abide having you sit all day in a maid's uniform. You're too pretty for that. Do you sew, Ilene?"

"Aye, Mrs. Phenwick, me mither taught me to stitch a fine seam. I make lace as well. Me fingers are agile."

"So is your mind, I can tell," Patricia returned. "There is one other question. Since you are Irish, I suspect you are a Catholic."

"'Tis nay so, Mrs. Phenwick," Ilene replied with a broad smile. "Me father is a descendant of th' Orangemen. His people were Anglicans. We're from the north of Ireland. Me mither was a Catholic as a garl, but when she married me da, she gave up her old faith. 'Twas love, you see. I'm unchurched. Me father forbade me mither to teach us Catholic ways. But she did tell me o' th' legends and tales o' th' Irish saints."

"Christian legends?"

"Aye, o' that—and o' th' fairies and other sprites that dwell in Ireland," Ilene returned.

"As I said, Aunt Patricia," Joseph interrupted, "Ilene has quite an imagination. One doesn't know where folklore leaves off and reality begins."

"Delightful," Patricia exclaimed. "Do you read, girl?"

"Aye, I told ye so. Don't you remember?"

"I meant, can you read aloud?"

"A bit. But I can learn."

"My eyes have become so tired it is difficult for me to see the print anymore," Patricia commented. "I dearly love to be read to. That will be one project we'll take on, teaching you to read aloud." The old woman brightened. "Now then, Marcia, Ilene is a bit smaller than you are. Surely you have some old frocks she can make over for herself. Something simple."

"There are closets full of unused dresses," Marcia declared. "And I'm certain Nancy has some. We'll see what we can find today."

"Does that mean that I get th' job?" questioned Ilene.

"Yes, child," Patricia said, motioning that she was dismissed. "You will begin tomorrow. You can get settled in today. Now, Joseph, are you going to examine me?"

Marcia took hold of Ilene's arm and guided her from the room.

Joseph took Patricia's wrist and felt for the pulsebeat.

"Do you like her, Joseph?"

"I beg your pardon."

"The girl—Ilene—do you find her attractive? I do. She's a pert young thing. Very lively."

"I must warn you, Aunt Patricia, she also has a very very lively imagination."

"All the better—all the better," the old lady said, settling back and gazing up into the round face of the young doctor. "Were I a man in your time of life, Joseph, I think I would find her most appealing." She lowered her eyelids and breathed deeply. "Ilene has the stuff of which I wish all the Phenwick women were made." Her eyes closed, then suddenly popped open. What had she said? A dim smile came to her lips.

Joseph was oblivious to her chatter as he took the count.

"Glory be, I can uncross me fingers now," Ilene exclaimed as they reached the hallway. "They were gettin' cramps in 'em, they were."

Marcia laughed. "I like you, Ilene. I hope we will become friends."

"Why should a highborn lady like you want to be friends with th' likes o' me?" Ilene questioned as she admired the other's pretty features.

"Funnily enough, Ilene," explained Marcia, "I was not highborn at all. I can remember a time when my dresses weren't near as nice as the one you're wearing. Then a miracle happened and I met a Phenwick woman. Before I knew it I was transformed into a fairy princess."

"You'll pardon me sayin', but from what I've seen o' fairy princesses, you're quite different," Ilene stated. "No offense. You have another kind of beauty. And there's no light that glows around you. And without wings—"

Marcia hugged the girl to her. "Oh, I like you, Ilene Dumphy! It's going to be a joy having you at Edward House. Don't bother fixing over my old dresses for now. I have one dress that is small for me. You can put that on and we'll go down and buy you a frock or two that will fit nicely to that fancy little figure of yours. Would you like that?"

"If I didn't know better," Ilene grinned, "I'd think I'd stepped right into fairyland."

"Come along," Marcia instructed, "your room will be on the third floor. It should be ready for you. And while you're settling your things, I'll go get the dress for you."

The room was small but adequate to the girl's needs. It was in the back part of the house so that she could look down on the garden.

"I've never been this high in th' air before," Ilene exclaimed. "It makes me dizzy to look down to th' ground. But I don't mind bein' dizzy. It makes it all th' more excitin'."

"I'll return in less than five minutes, Ilene," Marcia related. "You can slip out of those things.

There's water in the pitcher and you can use that basin."

Ilene closed the door behind Marcia and leaned against it. "Well, Moorduke, what do you think o' it? That's what I thought you would say, it's th' direction in which you've been pointin' me." She went to the bedpost and held out her finger to the small image she saw sitting there. "'Tis a step up I was wantin', but th' third floor was more than I counted on. You'll have to turn your head whilst I pull off me things. 'Tisn't proper for a gentleman, even a gentleman leprechaun to watch when a garl is takin' off her clothes." She giggled. "But seein' it's you, Moorduke, I'll leave it to your own choosin'."

CHAPTER FIVE

When Marcia arrived at Ilene's room with the attractive blue dress, she found the girl in a state of complete undress, merrily washing herself. She realized she had to return to the second floor and get a pair of pantaloons with a drawstring and other underthings. Ilene could never try on dresses with the ragged undergarments she owned.

"I washed once this mornin'," Ilene stated upon Marcia's return, "but I figured an extra scrub could do me nay harm."

"I brought along some sweet-smelling perfumē, Ilene," Marcia announced. "It will make you smell nice."

By then Ilene had stepped into the pantaloons and had them cinched about her waist. She applied the perfume in two dots on her breast. "Oh, 'tis th' scent o' roses. My second most favorite aroma."

"Put a little behind each ear," Marcia instructed. "What is your first most favorite aroma?"

"Violets."

"Violets?" A strange expression came to Marcia's face.

"In th' glen back in me homē near to Carrickfergus—that's where I was born," Ilene explained with animation, slipping into a petticoat

"I used to lie on th' green moss in th' summer and look ever so close at the wee Violet blossoms. Fact is, 'twas under a violet leaf I found—that is—some one sleepin'."

"Someone sleeping under a violet leaf?" Marcia questioned. "It must have been a very small person."

"Aye, he was that. And angry! Th' vile words he spouted were enough to make a vicar blush." She stared at Marcia's startled expression. "Ye nay believe me. 'Tis written on your face."

"You're a bright girl, Ilene. Do you believe what you just told me?"

"Aye, I do. You niver heard o' th' fairies that play in th' forest in Ireland?" asked Ilene, just as startled as Marcia at seeing the expression of disbelief.

"I've heard tales. And I've read stories," Marcia stated, trying to find the humor in the matter, "but I've never known—"

"I would like to introduce you to Moorduke," Ilene said. "He's sittin' on th' bedpost behind you."

Marcia leaped and pivoted about, controlling the shriek that wanted to come. "Where?"

"You can nay see him. Most folk can't. Isn't that so, Moorduke? He's nodding his head."

"Moorduke?" Marcia wore an expression of alarm.

"He's a leprechaun and I'm his person," Ilene tried to explain. "You see, I knocked over a mushroom in his fairy circle, which was addin' insult to injury after I disturbed his sleep under the violet pad. He said he was goin' to take me captive. And he's been with me ever since. I thought when I was eight years old and me mither told

49

me we was immigratin' to th' United States o'
America, that Moorduke would stay behind. Now
he's sorry he did nay. I was his prize and he
would nay let me escape from him. Me mither
says it's mainly children what see th' wee folk because adults are too big for 'em. It was hard for
her to believe that Moorduke was still with me."

Marcia gazed again at the bedpost. Then she
burst into laughter. "I'm beginning to understand."

"You are?"

"He's imaginary. I had an imaginary playmate
as a child. Her name was Drucilla," Marcia explained. "I haven't thought of her in years."

"Was your Drucilla a fairy?" asked Ilene in all
seriousness.

"No. She was like any other child to me."

"There, you see? It's not th' same thing. Moorduke is shakin' his head ... He says imaginary
playmates and fairies are two entirely different
things." Ilene had donned the dress.

"I'll not dispute that," Marcia said, feeling
uneasy. "I know little about either."

"And Moorduke says to tell you that leprechauns are not imaginary, they're as real as
you are. You've insulted him, you know."

"Tell him I'm sorry," Marcia stated.

"He heard you. He has ears. They're big
enough."

To change the subject. Marcia said, "The dress
is a little loose around the waist, but you well fill
out the bodice. Even loose it doesn't look badly
on you. We'll tie a bright ribbon sash about your
waist. Do you have a brush or a comb?"

"Nay, Mrs. Phenwick. I don't own such a
thing," Ilene answered. "Is me hair all tangles?"

"Come down to my room and we'll give it a good brushing," Marcia suggested. "And you can't wear those boots with a nice dress like that I'm certain to have an old pair of slippers you can wear."

Marcia took Ilene's hand and pulled her from the room. She stopped at the door and the girl ran into her. "And tell Moorduke to stay here. I don't want a leprechaun cluttering up my room."

"Oh, he's nay clutter . . . But he heard you and he'll amuse himself at somethin', won't you, Moorduke?"

Marcia shook her head and pulled the girl forward.

Nearly fifteen minutes later, her hair neatly fixed in a bun at the back of her head and straggly finger curls at each side of her face, Ilene was ready to embark on the shopping trip. The shoes were almost a perfect fit, tight only at the top of her foot. Marcia led her down to the first floor and took her into the ballroom, which was to the right of the foot of the stairs.

Ilene giggled with delight when she saw her reflection in the large mirrors around the walls of the room. "'Tis it really me?"

"It's really you, Ilene." Marcia laughed.

"Oh, I could hug you, Mrs. Phenwick," exclaimed the girl.

"Come ahead and do so." Marcia was that happy for Ilene. "And why don't you call me Miss Marcia, not Mrs. Phenwick."

"You'll nay mind?"

"Of course not."

Ilene's attention was attracted to the large portrait at the end of the room. "Who's that?"

51

"That's a likeness of the first Mrs. Phenwick. Mrs. Augusta Phenwick," Marcia informed.

"She was a very lovely lady, wasn't she?"

"Yes. I never knew her—not in person. That was painted a long time ago," Marcia explained.

Ilene moved closer to the portrait. "Oh, I think I'm goin' to like her. Wait until Moorduke gets a gander at her."

"Ilene—about Moorduke," Marcia said hesitatingly. "I think it best if you not mention him too often. Leprechauns will be very difficult to explain to Americans. Understand?"

"Aye, I know. 'Tis sad to have a friend you can nay share with others." She stared up into the face of the portrait. "Mrs. Augusta looks better back a ways, don't she?"

"There'll be other times for you to look at the paintings," Marcia explained. "We have things to do."

They went toward the door, Ilene constantly admiring her reflection as they moved.

"Are you certain that perfume was the aroma o' roses?"

"I beg your pardon." Marcia stopped and glanced back at the portrait. "Why do you ask?"

"For a moment there," Ilene returned, "I thought I whiffed th' smell o' violets. But it must be in me mind. I do have an imagination, as Dr. Ornby says."

Now Marcia stared deeply into Ilene's face. Unobtrusively she took a deep breath. "I'm wearing rose perfume, too. It's difficult to tell."

Ilene sniffed. "Aye, I was mistaken, 'tis roses I smell—now."

The shopping trip was successful. Not only did Marcia purchase three dresses suitable for Ilene to wear while she was attending to Patricia, but she also acquired two nicer dresses for her leisure hours. The entire adventure reminded her of the day she had first met Susannah Phenwick and that grand lady had bought finery for her. Somehow Marcia felt as if she were repaying a favor.

Marcia was sufficiently able to run the household at large Edward House, and she treated the servants with kindness and respect. She found people responded to a positive, pleasant attitude and ultimately she got more work accomplished with the people than she might have had she been more dictatorial in her approach. With Ilene she could not help but exude an element of friendliness that verged on familiarity. But Ilene was not like other servants, nor was she basically in that category.

Stella Murphy, on the other hand, did not possess a personality that invited closeness, especially with her employer. Marcia treated her with kindness and respect, but always held herself at a distance. The two attendants for Patricia were very different from each other. Stella was more involved with her young gentleman friend than she was with her work. Thoughts of him occupied many of her waking hours, which gave her a dreamy exterior. She did her work as required, but found she could sleep sitting up and she awakened at the drop of a feather.

Somehow Marcia felt a kind of rapport with Ilene she experienced with no other person in a position of servitude. They were like kindred spirits, old friends upon meeting. That friendship would surely grow through the years.

Stuart Phenwick without a doubt was the most handsome of all the Phenwick men in Boston. An ambitious businessman, he took life seriously, constantly aware of business matters and ways of improving the Medallion shipping interests. A man with good features and so magnificently proportioned, women and men stopped when he passed just to observe him. His charm was magnetic. All who beheld him were fascinated by that masculine beauty. Tailored to a fine degree, he chose attire that was both fashionable and colorful, preferring pastel hues as often as possible. Blues complemented him. He wore electric blue, especially in coats and vests during his informal hours. His trousers were always wrinkle-free, appearing as if he had just donned them brand-new. His clothing fit him when he walked as if it was precisely made to accentuate the marvelous physique beneath.

A member of an exclusive men's club in Boston, Stuart spent several hours each afternoon enjoying the recreation and the companionship of other businessmen, who found him to be a delight, a good sportsman and an interesting personality. Many would liked to have impressed him as a means of obtaining Phenwick money for backing in particular projects. While he appeared to find such individuals interesting, he claimed he was never in a position to distribute the family wealth without consulting other members. Still he was lavishly dined and entertained by opportunists who wished to get into his good favor.

Because the Phenwicks were once again becoming pinnacles of the social set in Boston, and Marcia was considered the grand lady to be wooed for her position, Stuart was also set upon by persons who were attempting to worm their way into the social scene. To be invited to a Phenwick party at Edward House was considered the zenith of achievement and indicated that one had become accepted among the elite of Boston. Consequently Stuart was aware that many persons who were not totally sincere were among his pretended admirers. But he had a way of laughing at himself and at others, for the games that people played amused him. Stalwart and honest in his approach to everyone with whom he came into contact, there was nothing artificial about him. He was himself a gentleman, and one who commanded and deserved the respect of all with whom he associated.

The handsome man arrived home that evening after spending two hours at the club. His appearance was always meticulous. Freshly shaved and barbered at that organization, and having enjoyed the athletics that were included as part of that club's activities, he radiated a magnetic glow, slightly flushed, robust. All of which underlined his comely youth.

Hearing voices in the parlor, Stuart went directly to that part of the house, where he found Marcia and Ilene examining the clothing which had been purchased that afternoon. He watched them without being observed for a short while before interrupting their girlish chatter.

"Don't tell me this is the same Ilene Dumphy I met yesterday " Stuart commented, with an admiring appraisal of the girl as he moved toward her. "What a transformation has taken place."

"You really think she has changed, my darling?" Marcia asked, noticing the glimmer of interest that shone in his eyes.

"She's perfectly attractive," Stuart replied circling halfway about the young lady.

"Go on with you! Sure now, I'm nay as pretty as all o' that," Ilene remarked. "'Tis a blush you're bringin' to me face."

"You mustn't mind the admiring observations of my husband, Ilene," Marcia said. "He has an eye for beauty. Don't you, my dear?"

"Occasionally," Stuart replied. "I wasn't aware that you had noticed, my precious Marcia."

"I try not to. Then you try not to observe when I find other persons attractive."

"We all have our little ways of amusing ourselves, haven't we?" Stuart commented. "I readily admit that I take pleasure in watching people. I do not limit such viewing to ladies; I find men interesting both in appearance and in attitude—certainly in intelligence. But I discover most persons who are unusual worth cultivating an interest in. It makes life more interesting. As for Ilene, she hardly resembles a girl who has come to work in the household."

"The dress she is wearing is one I purchased for special occasions when she is not attending to Grandmama," Marcia related. "It reminded me of years ago when Susannah took me and dressed me in the finery of a lady. I appreciated it. And if I'm returning the favor to Ilene, then I am happy to do so. She went to her husband, put her arms about his waist and held him close to her. "I love you, my darling. Do you mind if I was terribly extravagant in outfitting Ilene? I felt her natural Irish beauty should be augmented. Green is lovely with her coloring. Besides she told me of an occasion or two when she chanced up to Beacon Hill and was run off because of the poor way she was dressed. I certainly wouldn't want her running an errand and being put upon by dogs because she was not properly dressed for the neighborhood. A person has more respect for herself when she is nicely attired."

"Sure now, I don't know that I could be havin' more respect for meself," Ilene said, "if 'tis a matter o' me clothes. 'Tis but an outer dressin' for what is inside. B'gorra, 'tis nay that I'm any less a person than I am because o' th' clothes I wear. Still I suppose I look more respectable, and that's th' important thing, isn't it?"

"You look as if you belong on Beacon Hill, Ilene," Stuart commented. "Now then, I suppose we'll be having supper before long. Do I have time to change into something a little more comfortable, or are we dining formally tonight?"

"You may be as comfortable as you like, my darling, it's just the two of us," Marcia explained. "I'll help Ilene up with her things and give you a half hour before the meal will be served."

"Why don't you let me carry those things, my darling?" Stuart suggested. "You tell Cook I'll be ready to eat in thirty minutes. I want to stop in and say hello to Aunt Patricia before we dine. Won't you meet me in her room in fifteen minutes?"

"That's very kind of you," Marcia returned, looking from her husband to the sweet-faced Irish girl. "I'm certain Ilene will appreciate your help. I'll go instantly to the kitchen and advise Cook of your wishes, then meet you with Aunt Patricia."

Stuart let Ilene lead the way from the room. He carried the bundles, following her as she went up the stairs to the second floor, then on to the third. He could not help but notice the pert swish of her dress and the tempting movement of her hips as she climbed. Excitement in her walk, she seemed to dance up the stairs. When she finally reached the third floor and her room just beyond the stairway, she turned back to gaze appreciatively at the man.

" 'Tis a bit o' a climb, is it nay?" she asked, her eyes sparkling, her smile so vibrant it almost included an unspoken invitation.

"So this is your room?" Stuart commented. "Do you like it?"

"I've only been in it long enough to take a wash and change me clothes. Actually it was a dress Miss Marcia gave me to wear. I do believe it looks nice on me, although a bit large in th' waist. 'Tis a fine lady she is. I'm very proud to be working for her and Mrs. Phenwick."

"I'll just set them here on the bed," Stuart commented as he laid the garments down.

"Oooh, do be careful! You do nay wish to harm him, do you?" Ilene exclaimed.

"I beg your pardon?"

" 'Tis all right, he leaped outa th' way," Ilene related.

"I'm sorry. I don't quite follow what you're talking about."

" 'Tis nothin', Mr. Phenwick. I was just afraid you might—that is—that's fine—th' dresses are fine where they are. I wouldn't want you to change them."

"What's this about 'him' getting out of the way?"

"Ah, 'twas just me imagination, I guess," Ilene replied. "I have a way o' thinkin'—that is—you see, there's nay just th' two o' us in this room."

"Not just the two of us?"

"Nay, there's a third party, what's nay known to you, but he's very real to me, if you know what I mean."

"I confess I don't know, Ilene. What are you talking about?"

"Well, Mr. Phenwick—I don't suppose you believe in fairies, do you?" Ilene asked, a sincere expression on her face.

Stuart chuckled amusedly. "I can't say that I do. Then again, I can't say that I don't, Ilene. Do you?"

"Oooh, very much so, sar" she replied. "'Tis a fancy I have long had ever since I was a wee garl back in Ireland. O' course, 'tis different there. Many people believe in th' wee folk and th' little people who play in th' glen."

"I recall speaking to a Chauncy or a Patrick or something or other—one of the dockhands who seemed to put great stock in the little people. Whenever a mishap would occur, he would say that a leprechaun had caused it."

"Oh, leprechauns don't always cause accidents or do vile things," Ilene protested. "As a matter o' fact, they're really quite good little people—but mischievous, I must say that for them. They do have their way o' playin' little pranks. But you have to be on th' good side o' them, you do."

"I see. And are you on the good side of leprechauns?"

"Well, I am as far as Moorduke is concerned," she said before she caught herself.

"Moorduke?"

"I didn't mean to say that. But now that it's out, I suppose I might as well fess up. I happen to belong to a leprechaun who's cum with me from Ireland."

"Ilene, I love your sense of humor." Stuart laughed loudly.

"I did nay say that to be funny, sar," Ilene explained. "As a matter o' fact I said it because it's th' truth."

"You'll pardon me if I find it amusing," Stuart remarked, attempting to control his laughter. "Since I've never encountered a leprechaun, I don't know that I can put much faith in their reality."

"Were you to know Moorduke, you'd put faith in him," Ilene protested. "I've known him to do weird things. 'Tis strange th' way he acts. He's so possessive, you know? He looks after me."

"Is he on the bed?" Stuart questioned, curiously looking to where he had set the garments a few minutes before.

"Aye, he was there a minute ago, but he leaped away. He did nay wish to be buried beneath th' clothing."

"I would be curious to meet him someday," Stuart said patronizingly.

"Well, Moorduke is very exclusive. He doesn't make himself visible to most people. 'Tis a peculiarity he has," Ilene said. " 'Tis his way o' protectin' himself. He says because most people do nay believe in leprechauns, he would be foolish to try to explain who he is. Therefore, he makes himself invisible."

"How can he make himself invisible to me and not to you?" Stuart questioned.

"I don't know how he does it. Sure now, but he does it, though. 'Tis a fact. Even me brothers and sisters do nay see him. He says it's because he

fears one o' th' b'ys may pull some prank on him,
b'ys bein' what they are."

Stuart laughed. Still he could not deny the serious expression Ilene wore and the deep belief she
must have in this mysterious Moorduke. For a moment he thought of his brother, Gordon, and his
devout faith in religion. Why did he equate Ilene
with Gordon? Was it that factor of sincere belief
that made them seem parallel in his mind? He
himself did not have the religious convictions of
his brother, nor had he ever. When it came to the
matter of faith, he was confused. Therefore he put
belief in his fellow man and trusted there was a
God somewhere who was keeping the earth in
working order. Disillusionment had persuaded
him that the fanatical religion that Gordon
espoused was not for him. Nor had he taken it
seriously when his mother had carried on about
religion during his younger years. Why would
someone of a primitive superstitious nature such as
Ilene possessed not put faith in a leprechaun?
Perhaps she had a sixth sense that made Moorduke visible to her and not to himself. Maybe that
is what all religion was about, a sixth sense that
had to do with spiritual awareness. It was a subject he had long considered and only in passing
had mentioned to such persons as John Collier
and Marcia. At the present point in his life, he
was not convinced of anything for certain. Perhaps that was a missing ingredient that he would
someday discover.

"My wife is waiting for me, Ilene. If you ask
your Moorduke politely one day he might allow
me to meet him. I should like that," Stuart said as
he reached the door. He nodded slightly. "You
will spend your first day with Aunt Patricia to-

morrow. We won't see each other until tomorrow evening. In that case, I wish you welcome to Edward House. Furthermore, if it's all the same, I welcome your Moorduke, too." He smiled congenially as he left the room, closing the door gently behind him.

Ilene stood a moment looking after the man and at the closed door. Then she put her hands about the knob on the bedpost and swung herself around in a half circle. "Well, what do you think o' that, Moorduke? Oooh, you do, do you? Well now, he's already taken by th' mistress o' th' house. And I'm nay about to do anything crazy to jeopardize me position here. And I'll have none o' your shenanigans in th' matter either."

Ilene glanced again toward the doorway, then back at the little creature she saw now mounted on the bedpost. "But I must say he *is* a fair handsome man. 'Twould be a miracle if one day I were to meet one half as pleasant as he who is not taken. O' course there is Dr. Ornby, who is a fine man. But I don't think he takes that much o' a fancy to me. The truth is, I believe he's interested in me sister, Sheila. I would be th' last person in th' world to interfere with me sister's happiness. You do understand, don't you, Moorduke? I thought you would. And you do understand that I can nay make flirtatious glances at a married man who is th' master o' th' house. 'Twould nay be me place. But I can admire him from a distance, which will be just fine with me. Ah, Moorduke, you've got to give me encouragement that there'll be another as nice as he is. And you should nay suggest that I would take an interest in Mr. Phenwick in that kind o' way. Although I must say, it could be easy to lose me heart to such a man as he."

CHAPTER SIX

Stella Murphy's hours for sitting with Patricia Phenwick were from seven o'clock at night until seven in the morning, leaving the other twelve hours for Ilene. Since she was up at dawn and often awake before sunrise, Ilene was well prepared by seven to take her position with the old lady.

At the door to Patricia Phenwick's room, Ilene met Stella.

"Sure now, she's still asleep. Been asleep all night. Slept like a baby, she did," the somewhat attractive night attendant said. "'Twas a long night. But I suppose I'll get used to it. This way I have time for me man, Bill Cockle, during th' day hours. Since he works at night, 'tis just as well we both have th' same hours."

"Is there anything I should know about Mrs. Phenwick?" Ilene asked.

"I know little or nuthin'. She goes to sleep by eight o'clock at night— sometimes nay until nine. She doesn't say much. She seems very tired," Stella explained. "She coughs a bit and has difficulty goin' to sleep. Once she dozes off, she seems to sleep quite comfortably. I don't know what th' concern is. I suppose 'tis necessary to have around-th'-clock watch because o' her age."

"Is it—I mean, does she talk to you much?" Ilene asked.

"Sure now, she said a word or two. It's mostly ramblin' about her family that uses up her words," Stella replied. "I do nay read, so I can nay pacify her that way. Last night th' other Mrs. Phenwick and Mr. Phenwick came in and sat with her for a while. Then they left at about eight-thirty. 'Twas kinda pitiful because she went on about how it was when she was a garl. She knew how young people were. Oh, she's very happy that the other Mrs. Phenwick is goin' to have a wee one. Yet on 'tother hand, she ain't so sure she wants to be a great-grandmother."

"I'll try nay to mention it to her," Ilene said. "I don't suppose we'll ever have time for you and me to have much o' a chat, will we?"

"No other than when we're cumin' on or goin' off work," Stella replied, "unless o' an evenin' and I kin sneak out for a few minutes. I don't know that that would be a good idea. The doctor says as how she might cum down with a coughin' fit at any time and will need someone to pat her on th' back and sit her up."

"Well then, Stella, I will see you later. 'Tis best I get in with her."

"As I say she's still sound asleep, and probably won't wake for another hour. But then there's nay tellin', is there?"

Ilene entered the room cautiously, tiptoeing so as not to awaken the old lady, who was propped up on two pillows. Had Patricia not been breathing heavily, she might have appeared as a corpse. The girl crept to get a closer observation of the woman. The draperies were drawn at the windows, with only a crack of light coming in where they parted. The scent of old age and gloom was present. After a brief examination, Ilene went back to a large chair which had been brought in especially for the attendant. It was comfortable and she settled into it, as relaxed as she could be under the circumstances.

For an hour, Ilene gazed about the room examining various articles, the paintings: the small portrait of handsome Edward Phenwick and a portrait of Elias Phenwick, the old woman's first and second husbands. She was attracted to the large, beautifully framed portrait of Marcia, opposite the bed. Turning around, she saw the painting of Kate, Patricia's other granddaughter, which had recently been completed. Other paintings, mostly landscapes, were hung about the room, a collection that Patricia had gathered over the years and which were created by the artists whom she had sponsored. Without her patronage they would not have become successful. Other objects of interest were in the room—books on shelves, seven thin prominent volumes between bookends on a table near the window. Ilene went to examine those, to discover they were the books of poetry Patricia Phenwick had written. The poems were dated and, according to the girl's calculations, some were at least fifty years old. She realized she would have to learn to read better and take the opportunity to get to know the old lady through her poetic writings.

Ilene also found a large book on a small table entitled *The Mysteries of Rosea Hackleby*. Intrigued, she leafed through the volume with the strange chapter titles: Witchcraft, Reincarnation, Possession, Black Magic, Superstitions, Metaphysics. Perhaps later in the day, when Mrs. Phenwick was napping, she would take the opportunity to look more closely at that book. Something about it fascinated her. Most of the titles were words she knew nothing about, if she knew the words at all.

Patricia's eyes opened as if she were suddenly aroused from a dream. They glanced about the room, and came to rest on the figure of Ilene sitting on the large chair.

"Is that you, Stella?" Patricia asked, her old eyes watery as she tried to focus them. "I would like a glass of water, if you don't mind."

"'Tis nay Stella, 'tis me, Ilene," the girl said, rising and going to the bed.

"My goodness! Can this be the same waif who came in only yesterday looking a bundle of rags and tatters?" Patricia asked.

"Aye, 'tis me. Miss Marcia took me shoppin' for new clothes. I must admit I do feel like another person. Sure now, I seem real elegant, I do," Ilene announced.

"Pull back the draperies. Let's have a little daylight in here," Patricia ordered. "I'm not dead yet and I want to see as much of this earth as there is left for me to see—even if it's only from my bed."

Ilene did as she was told, letting sunlight into the room. The brightness was almost too much for the old lady, who shielded her eyes momentarily until they adjusted to the glare. "Let me look at you. I find it difficult to believe you are the same person."

"Aye, 'tis me all right, Mrs. Phenwick, I've just got fancy on th' outside is all."

"We must do something about that brogue of yours," Patricia remarked. "While it's attractive in a provincial way, it indicates a lack of education."

"'Tis th' truth, I'm nay educated well at all,"

Ilene explained. "In fact, I've had nay proper schooling."

"While I have no desire to make you over," Patricia stated, "I do feel that a person—if she is to get anywhere in this world—must better herself as much as she possibly can. If I can in any way help you do that, it will be my privilege to do so."

"Why would you want to do that?"

"Because you're a human being, my dear," the old lady commented, "and I've long had a great respect for the human race. I've contributed what I could, and I've taken what I could. Now as I come to the last lingering moments and I feel myself withering every day, I would like to have another project. Projects have always kept me going. I like to be accomplishing things, to be achieving. If I can help you to raise yourself from the poverty in which you were raised, then I would be accomplishing something worthwhile. The only way you can acquire such elevation, my dear, is to improve yourself, to pull yourself up by your bootstraps, as it were, and teach yourself to become a lady."

"Sure now, I don't know how I could do that. I've nay trainin' in bein' a lady whatsoever. Nor would I know what to do if I were one," said Ilene.

"Bring a cloth and wash my face," Patricia returned, "and we will discuss the matter of your education. It seems to me that you would be far better off in this life if you were to learn more about being you."

"Sure now, I know enough about bein' me. That's all I am is me."

"Yes, you no doubt know about the you that you are right now," Patricia remarked, "but I should imagine it would be difficult for you to meet a proper young gentleman to help you through life."

"To help me through life?"

"I mean a husband. Every young girl should work toward finding the right mate. For to go through life alone can be a very dismal thing. A girl who has never married is to be pitied. Even though a married girl may lose her husband through an early death, at least she has memories of happiness. You cannot buy happiness, my dear nor friendship. You achieve both of those by being attractive—not only physically beautiful, which you are—but if you have no intellect to go with it, you cannot hope to attract a man who is anything but a dullard like yourself. I am not saying that you are dull, my child, but without education or refinement, you will go through life attracting only unrefined people. It has long been a belief of mine that we attract to ourselves that which we are. If we are intelligent, we attract intelligent people; if we're stupid, we attract the same. I've seen this time and time again. I had a rather dull nephew, who attracted an equally dull wife. Fortunately both of their sons did not turn out to be as dull as they were. My nephew Stuart was one of those boys. Because of certain intervention by members of the family, he is accomplished at being a gentleman, whereas his brother, Gordon, is quite the opposite. I sometimes worry about Gordon. With all his knowledge he is a lost sheep. How can I become so philosophical so early in the morning?" She sighed. "You will run downstairs and tell Cook I am ready for breakfast. Then we'll get about the routine of things, won't we?"

Patricia had developed the custom of reciting the family history several hours a day for Marcia to record, which she did meticulously. After taking notes for two to three hours, Marcia would leave the old lady and go to her own chamber, where she would compile the notes. The next day she would begin by reading what she had written to Patricia. During that time Ilene was always present, listening. The girl found a deep fascination in the machinations of the Phenwick clan, in all the intrigues and intensities that had led these people to a life of opulence and grandeur. A mysterious undercurrent lingered and often played a significant role, a bizarre element running through the thread of the story. The ghostly presence of Augusta Phenwick seemed to play a persuasive hand from the other side of life over her heirs.

Ilene heard of the terrorizing jeopardy in which many of the Phenwick women had discovered themselves. She shuddered in response to the tales the old lady related. She was deeply moved by Patricia's story of herself, her two husbands, her two daughters and her son, who was killed during the War of 1812. She enjoyed hearing of Patricia's grandness as a lady of society, a poetess and a woman highly involved with the arts, a subject about which Ilene knew very little. As the days came and went, the girl felt as if she were beginning to know the Phenwick family.

When Marcia was away writing, or going about her own business, the old lady would draw Ilene out time and time again in conversation, wanting to know more about her. What were her thoughts, her way of life? For some reason Ilene presented a challenge to the old woman to assist as best she could in altering Ilene's circumstances.

"But why should you want to do that, Mrs. Phenwick?" Ilene asked. "Sure now, I was born o' a poor family. I've nay grand ambitions about meself for certain."

"My dear child, a person who has no grand ambitions may as well be dead as far as I'm concerned," Patricia uttered. "Grand ambitions are what make life worth living."

"If I have any, they've been kept to meself," Ilene said. "O' course I've confided them in Moorduke—I mean—"

"I beg your pardon."

"I was—uh—sayin'—I've confided me ambitions to meself only."

"I thought you mentioned a name."

The blood drained from Ilene's face. Up to that time she had made a point of never broaching the subject of Moorduke to the old lady. It had slipped out.

"Well, I may have but—uh—I meant nothin' by it."

"Was the name Moorduke?" Patricia asked.

"Aye, that was th' name," Ilene answered too quickly. "I mean, well, b'gorra, I nay meant to tell you about Moorduke."

"Who is this Moorduke? Do you have a gentleman friend you've been concealing from me?"

"Nay, he is nay a gentleman, that is, he is a gentleman but he's— Oh dear, I don't know how to explain Moorduke to anybody. When I tell them th' truth, they think I'm prevaricatin', I know."

"Prevaricating? Creating a story about an imaginary man?"

"I don't know as how he's an imaginary man.

He's nay a man at all," Ilene said with a slight laugh.

"Then he must be imaginary if he's not a man—unless he's a boy," Patricia stated.

"To tell you the truth, he's neither man nor b'y. He's— Oh, I can't tell you, Mrs. Phenwick. You'll find me silly, I'm afraid. It seems most people do when I mention Moorduke to them. They laugh. But because you can nay see somethin' doesn't mean that it don't exist."

"Can you explain yourself?" inquired Patricia.

"In the first place, Moorduke is a—well, he's a wee person."

"A wee person."

"If you can call him a person. I do, because he seems a person to me," Ilene explained. "He has two eyes, a nose, a mouth, legs, arms, hands, everythin'."

"This Moorduke—who or what precisely is he?" Patricia questioned. "I assure you that I will not laugh at your explanation, my dear."

"Very well, I'll tell you. But I don't think you'll much care for me answer. Moorduke is a—leprechaun. He's followed me from Ireland."

"A leprechaun?"

"Aye. He's quite small. But he's very real to me," Ilene explained. "He's great company. I know others do nay see him—or if they do, they pretend they don't."

"But you see him, is that it?" Patricia asked.

"Aye, Mrs. Phenwick, 'tis true. I do see Moorduke. I talk to him and he talks to me. Sometimes he gets a little annoyed at what I have to say, or what I do, and he lets me have it."

"Fascinating!" Patricia exclaimed. "I have heard a legend or two about leprechauns, but I've never encountered anyone who has actually met one."

"It was all by accident, I assure you," Ilene said. "It was his doin', nay me own. Although he does blame me for knockin' over one o' his mushrooms. He's nay *my* leprechaun, I'm *his* person. He came over with me, now he's afraid to go back. So I'm sorta stuck with him."

"Have you told Dr. Ornby about this?" inquired Patricia.

"Aye. He laughed too. 'Tis nay to be believed by most. Yet I can nay deny me senses. If he is only in me imagination, he certainly has a way o' expressin' himself."

"Where is this Moorduke now?" Patricia asked, leaning forward as her curiosity rose.

"At this very minute? You'll laugh at me if I tell you," Ilene replied. "You see, he's sittin' on th' bedpost."

"Good heavens! I had no idea that we were being overheard," Patricia exclaimed. "What is he doing there?"

"He's just lookin' at you. It's a good omen that he's cum in, because he doesn't like most people. He leaps outa sight if he doesn't like a person at all. But he's been in many times to watch you. He just sorta appears. Don't you, Moorduke? He says that is th' case, and that you're a dunderhead if you don't believe it."

"Me? A dunderhead? Patricia reacted indignantly. "Well, in that case, I must believe in him, mustn't I?"

"When I was a wee garl, I recall seein' many fairies—particularly in th' glen when I would go out by meself. I told me mither about it. And she would say, 'Aye, 'tis fairies you've been watchin'.

They've put a prettiness in your face.' She always blamed th' fairies for me beauty."

"Did your mother believe in fairies?"

' "Oooh, I do believe so," Ilene answered. "She said it was a good omen that I should meet up with the fairies when I was a small child, because they would put a fairy crown upon me head. And one day I would grow up to be somebody important. I guess I've nay grown up yet, because I'm nay somebody important. One o' these days I will be. When that happens, I'll have th' fairies to thank for it—and Moorduke here."

Patricia stifled a chuckle. "What sort of important person do you wish to be, Ilene?"

"Most o' all I should like to be a grand lady, and live in a castle maybe, or a mansion, and have nice finery and jewels."

"You're a dreamer, Ilene Dumphy, that's what you are."

"Aye, that I am. There's nay denyin' that. I never said I weren't. B'gorra, if I don't believe in fairies, then nothin' will happen to me—th' same as with everyone else. I rather think that life is o' more importance than that. Don't you, Mrs. Phenwick?"

Now Patricia could not hold back the laughter. "I believe you, Ilene. I'm not laughing at you, but at your delivery, which I find amusing. I recall when I was a very young girl, I used to have an imaginary playmate myself. We were good friends in childhood. But she disappeared."

"I had an imaginary playmate, too," Ilene expressed. "I knew he was imaginary. His name was O'Ryan. He used to be around me all th' time. He would show me some o' th' most unusual things. And I would say, 'O'Ryan, you're pullin'

73

me leg by talkin' such a way.' And O'Ryan would turn to me and say, 'Aye, Ilene, old garl, you'll learn someday.' But O'Ryan disappeared when I was still a wee garl. He just up and left one day. That was before th' time I met Moorduke."

"Moorduke took O'Ryan's place, is that what you're trying to say?" Patricia questioned, enjoying the situation.

"I suppose there are those who think that is th' case," Ilene responded. "But I know O'Ryan was imaginary. Moorduke, he is somethin' else. He is nay at all like O'Ryan. O'Ryan was mostly in me imagination. I would see him when I would close me eyes. Ah, I know you don't understand me and th' little people, do you?"

"I don't say that I believe in fairies, Ilene, yet I don't say that I don't. If they're very real to you let them remain so. Don't deny them. You have attracted them for a reason."

"Oooh, th' regular fairies I don't attract anymore—just Moorduke," Ilene said, turning her attention to the bedpost. "He says that leprechauns are nay fairies, although they do be kin."

"If that's the case, what is Moorduke doing here?" Patricia asked.

"He cum because he wanted to be with me," Ilene related, "because I am his person. I know I'm nay makin' much sense, and I do wish I could explain it better. Sometimes it perplexes me, but I can nay deny me senses, can I?"

"In that large book on the small table, *The Mysteries of Rosea Hackleby*," Patricia stated, "there is a chapter about little people, fairies and that sort of thing. To Rosea Hackleby they were real: forms of spirits, but of another world. I recall reading it and laughing to myself, thinking that the old girl had become peculiar when she wrote about them. I do remember she wrote that very few people ever see them because they don't want to. I think that is the case with me. I don't really want to see such creatures, because they would go against my sense of reality. But to you— and I love you for it, Ilene—your sense of reality involves a certain touch of whimsy and fantasy. If Moorduke is real to you, then God bless you for it. Enjoy him as long as you can. However, I have a premonition that one day he will go away."

"He'll nay go away without me. He's afraid to go back to Ireland—or even to England. He could make his way from there. It's the ship-crossin' that worries him," Ilene explained. "If I were to go back, maybe he might go along and find his way back to th' glen where his fairy ring is, where his own kind are."

"I have a feeling that you will return across the sea, because you will find a kind of happiness in a man of human proportions that will take your romantic image of Moorduke away and no longer make it necessary for him to be with you."

"Do you mean he'll be replaced by a real man?" Ilene questioned. "Is that what you're tryin' to tell me?"

"Yes, my child. When true love comes to you, you will no longer need the fantasy of other-worldly people. You will discover a new dimension in your life where the romantic fantasies are no longer needed. An exquisite happiness will come over you."

Ilene glanced at the bedpost. She stared for a moment, then looked back at the old lady. "I think Moorduke believes you."

CHAPTER SEVEN

Spring was in full bloom that midafternoon when the huskily built young man came striding up the hill. Dressed in black, he moved in a self-assured manner. His round face was flushed and he paused once or twice along the way to catch his breath, for the upward climb was not part of his usual way of life. Of average height, his chunky appearance made him seem larger than he actually was.

He paused before he turned into the gate at Edward House, staring up at the large mansion as he took a handkerchief and blotted his forehead. Heavy eyebrows shaded his fiercely intense dark eyes. His features were more ordinary than handsome. His corpulent appearance gave him a look of overindulgence. Puffy cheeks. Thick lips. Pudgy hands with short fingers. Trudging forward, he hesitated a moment at the top of the steps to catch his breath and adjust his clothing before he reached to pull the doorbell.

Well composed by the time Dietrich opened the door, he stared a moment at the butler as if he expected the tall man to step aside and immediately permit him to enter.

"Oh, Reverend Phenwick, it's you," the stately butler commented upon recognition of the man.

"Won't you come in? I will tell Mrs. Phenwick that you are here."

"That is not necessary, Dietrich," Gordon Phenwick replied. "I will go up to see my aunt without being announced."

"You'll pardon me, sir, I cannot allow that," the butler said in his heavy Germanic accent. "Mrs. Phenwick has given strict orders that she is not to be interrupted by anyone without their first being announced, including the doctor or any member of her family."

"Very well, Dietrich, announce me."

Gordon Phenwick waited in the foyer while the obliging servant went upstairs to announce his arrival. A few minutes later Dietrich returned, moving all the way down the stairs before informing Gordon that his aunt would see him in five minutes.

"How tiresome," Gordon commented, pulling a large gold watch from his vest pocket.

Dietrich excused himself and left the young preacher to his own devices. Gordon paced. He did not like to wait. Especially he did not like to wait at Edward House, which he was convinced was corrupt with a past of sin and illicit happenings. During his wait, he went into the ballroom to gaze at his reflection in one of the large mirrors. His black attire, highlighted only by a white shirt, gave him an austere appearance. The buttons of his vest were slightly bulging. He sucked in his stomach in hopes of seeming less overabundant. That gesture did little to alter his appearance. Examining his watch again, he decided that sufficient time had passed. Glancing at the portrait of Augusta Phenwick, he widened his eyes as was part of his practiced expression when lecturing to the sinful of Boston.

A few minutes later, after he had regained his breath at the top of the stairs, Gordon rapped gently on the door and entered. He looked about, catching only a brief glimpse of Ilene as she sat in the chair provided for her. It had been pushed back to make room for another chair to be drawn forward where the guest might sit.

"Gordon, I rather imagined you'd be coming one of these days," Patricia said as she sat propped in the bed with extra pillows behind her back.

"Aunt Patricia, I have come," Gordon stated, "because of a disturbing dream I had last night. Nay, a prophetic dream, I believe. In my dream an angel of the Lord came down to me and said that, while I was spending much time addressing the poor misfits and sin-filled souls of the streets, I was neglecting the salvation of a member of my own family. Furthermore, the angel explained that I should come to Edward House. I realized it could be my brother, Stuart, whom I was being directed to save. I know that he has long turned a deaf ear. I continue to pray for his salvation nevertheless."

"Then you've decided it's *my* salvation you were directed to seek. Is that the case, Gordon?" inquired Patricia. "If it is, I suggest that you are barking up the wrong tree."

"May I sit, Aunt Patricia?" Gordon asked. "I did not mean to distress you with my announcement. I have been meaning to come to call on you anyway, realizing that you are bed ridden and no doubt in dire need of company."

"True, I am bed ridden," Patricia returned. "I

am not in dire need of anything—except the one thing you cannot possibly give me and that is youth. I have spent all of mine. It is gone. I'm in declining years. There was a time when I thought I would like to live forever, before the infirmity of old age set in. Now, no longer my glorious self, but a creature confined to this one little room, my lust for life has diminished greatly. I am ready to endure whatever may lie ahead."

Gordon got to his knees beside the bed and clasped his hands together in a prayerlike pose. "I will pray for you, Aunt Patricia. Will you join me?"

"Get off your knees, boy," Patricia commanded. "I do not care for you to pray and go through your religious histrionics at my bedside."

"Then that which you must endure," Gordon stated, "surely will be in the depths of hell . . . in the fiery furnaces of Lucifer. You must seek your salvation if you would go to that heavenly place and be among the holy of holies."

"I said get off your knees. I don't want you praying at my bedside, Gordon Phenwick. Just as I never wanted your mother, Lillian, praying over me," Patricia stated in no uncertain terms. "My salvation is quite frankly none of your business— whatever salvation might be."

"But my business is salvation, for I am about the Lord's work. I am ordained to preach the gospel and to save the sinners, wretched as they may be, from the blazing holocaust of hell!"

"By what authority do you claim to know about hell?" questioned Patricia. "Now get up this instant or I shall summon Dietrich and have you thrown out of here!"

Disgruntled, Gordon rose to his feet and stood

with his eyes widened, that fierce expression glaring down into his aunt's face. "I know of the fiery terror of hell, because it is written about in the Bible. I have been directed by the angel of the Lord himself to come here this very day in hope of bringing about your eternal salvation. Oh, it would horrify me to think that my own aunt had gone to such a perdition as you must be headed for."

"What makes you think I am headed anywhere?" Patricia inquired, folding her hands together and cracking the knuckles as she did so.

"You're an old woman, Aunt Patricia. The life you have led has not been saintly," Gordon explained. "I know of the riotous way you've lived, of the men with whom you've consorted, of the parties, of the debauchery! Oh, without salvation you will surely be among those who roast in the flames! I can hear the cries of the torment now!" He clenched his fist and raised it to his head. "I can hear the shrieks of terror, the horror as flesh is being consumed by fire! The agony of the damned as they flounder about in that flaming inferno! The screams of the wicked, the evildoers, the licentious, the lustful, those who have been ravaged by sin, have delighted in the taste of the flesh unconsummated by the church, living against the holy word! I see them now: flames consuming souls and shrieks of the anguished deafening the ears!"

Ilene, who had been cowering in the large chair, suddenly let out a scream of alarm. "No, no! 'Tis nay so. Mrs. Phenwick will nay burn in such flames!"

Gordon cast a quick, furious glance in the direction of the girl. His eyes were ablaze with zealousness and rage. "Oooh, sinners! Repent! Repent, for the day of judgment is at hand!"

"Get out of here, Gordon! Get out this instant! Or I shall immediately summon Dietrich! Do you hear me?"

"You cannot turn me out until you have heard what I have to say!" Gordon hollered. "I know—I know about you, Patricia Phenwick. I know about the men. I know about the terrible sinful life you have led. I know of the inglorious end you will surely meet unless you repent of your ways!"

"Get out! Get out!" Patricia exclaimed as firmly as she could, reaching for for the cord to call the butler.

"Oh, Aunt Patricia, I will pray for you. Even my prayers will not undo the terrible things you have done in your lifetime."

"I've done no terrible things. I have lived as I was meant to live," Patricia explained. "Get out of here or I shall forbid you ever to enter this house again. If you do come back, I want to hear no more of this outrageous declamation of yours. Now get out."

The door opened and Dietrich appeared. He was a good head taller than Gordon, appearing a towering giant beside the preacher. "You rang for me, Mrs. Phenwick?"

"I want you to escort Reverend Phenwick to the front door, if you please," Patricia declared.

"Oh, woman of sin, confess—confess this day! Your minutes are numbered in this life. Proclaim your Jesus Christ before it is too late!"

Dietrich put his large hand on the man's arm. With a forceful tug, he practically propelled Gordon from the room.

Ilene was crying, she had become so terrified. As Gordon left, she rose and went to the bed.

"There there, child. Pay no heed to Gordon; he is a fanatic like his mother. He wants to scare people. I know what he's up to. He wants to scare me into giving a large amount of money to his church. He's been after me before. Now he must feel my termination is at hand. Well, I'll show him a thing or two. Will you be so kind as to go and fetch Marcia?"

Ilene quickly left the room, doing her best to contain the sobs jerking within her. Once the girl was gone, with great effort Patricia raised herself from the bed, put her feet to the side and rose. Grasping various objects she made her way to the table where the brandy decanter was kept. With trembling hands she poured herself part of a glass and quickly downed it. Mustering strength, she moved as quickly back to the bed as she could. Brandy had been forbidden her. With effort, she was back in the bed under a light linen covering before Ilene returned with Marcia.

"What is all the excitement, Grandmama?" Marcia asked, going directly to the bed.

"It was Gordon. He came in here like the wild man he is at times, insisting on my salvation, beseeching me to confess Jesus Christ as my savior. Well, I had him ejected from the place. Dietrich is powerful enough to handle him, I am certain. I confess he alarmed me."

"Alarmed you, Grandmama?"

"Yes." She tried to chuckle but it caught in her throat. "Not about the eventuality of what happens beyond this life, rather of the nearness of my approaching demise. He made it painfully clear that that time is near."

"Nonsense, Grandma*ma*. Joseph says you are coming along fine as long as you remain in your bed," Marcia said.

"Joseph said—he's a doctor, isn't he?" Patricia commented. "May I please have a glass of water? I seem to have something caught in my throat."

Marcia quickly got a glass of water and helped Patricia take a few sips.

"Thank you," Patricia sighed. "I know the days are growing fewer and fewer for me. I have never been able to swallow that kind of philosophy that Gordon preaches and his mother preached before him. I do not believe that death is the end of all. Far from it. This mind, or personality, spirit, whatever it may be called, goes on. Of that I have long been convinced. Augusta has persuaded me that there is something beyond this. My second husband, Elias, who was a minister, was set in his opinions, although not as severely as Gordon is. I always put faith in something far less mysterious and overwhelming than the fabled fires of hell the church seems to know so well. Nor do I put stock in that allegorical heavenly paradise, or in angels and archangels and goodness knows who else flapping around in pious poses and playing eternal harps. No. No, I will not accept that theory at all. What frightens me is the awareness that there is so little time left for me in this earthly house. Still when I stop to think, I realize I have accomplished much and will accomplish a bit more before I finish with this tired flesh. It amazes me when I consider the circumstance of growing old and being filled with pain. It is as if my soul wants to be lifted out. This body has endured as much torment as it has needed to experience. It's not dying I dread, but the inevitable thought of leaving all this that has been gloriously mine in a lifetime of opulence and fortune. Will it continue? I don't know. But more and more I become curious of what may be yonder."

"Grandma*ma*, I don't like to hear you speak of such things," Marcia said, holding tightly to the old lady's hand.

"There are things we must confront, my dearest Marcia. Death is one of them. If it distresses you to speak of this, we will not," Patricia sighed. "I'm fatigued. Gordon exhausted me. I believe it is time for me to take a nap. What a comfort it is to have you with me, Marcia. I feel so peaceful when you hold my hand like this that I feel whatever will transpire another hand will reach out and touch mine when the time for transition takes place— just as you are holding it at this moment."

Marcia kissed the old lady's hand. She rose to remove two of the pillows supporting her. "Grandma*ma*, isn't it uncomfortable for me to be sitting on the bed beside you?"

"I like to have you here."

Ilene, who had been observing from the far side of the room, slowly moved toward the bed. She wore an enigmatic smile, yet a frightened expression came to her face as she seemed to want to express what was on her mind. "Would you be excusin' me if I interrupted for a moment?"

"What is it, child?" Patricia questioned, glancing up into the beautiful face. It was somehow filled with an expression of wonder.

"Moorduke asked me to give you something."

"I beg your pardon?"

"He just now brought me a bouquet of violets. He said I was to give them to you. Glory be, I don't know where he got violets, but he's forever surprisin' me with strange gifts and violets are one o' his favorites." She held forth an empty hand. "Funny, I thought there were violets there. It seems to me there should be for I have a very strong fragrance o' violets around me."

Patricia smiled, holding out her hand to accept the invisible violets. "My dear girl, I do believe you have violets for me. I accept them. Give my thanks to Moorduke, if you will. They are a token of reassurance, an omen of good, I have no doubt whatsoever."

Marcia stared at Ilene as she watched Patricia accept the invisible bouquet. Then she looked a question into Patricia's eyes. The old lady smiled and held her hand toward her nose as if to smell the fragrance. She smiled sweetly, gently putting her hand down to her side.

"Does Moorduke accept my thanks?"

"Yes, he's very happy for you, Mrs. Phenwick. He says you know what they mean."

Marcia's mouth sagged as she swallowed hard. "Do they mean—?"

Patricia said, "Whatever violets are meant to mean." She closed her eyes, relaxed, sighing before she gently drifted off into slumber.

Marcia held her hand for several minutes until she realized the woman was fast asleep. Then she released her hold. Rising from the bed, she gazed strangely into Ilene's warm expression. She did not speak, but slowly backed toward the door until she stood at the threshold and stared back into the room. Had she imagined it, too? Or had she very definitely perceived the scent of violets?

CHAPTER EIGHT

The blossoms of spring had fallen from the trees. New leaves had obtained full growth and had become dark green. The sounds of laughter drifted through the warm air. Birds chattered noisily in treetops instructing their young. The clothes of winter had been packed away. Even the spring apparel was being modified for the warmth of the approaching summer. Gaiety laughed about the streets. Children were more mischievous than they had been in earlier months. Young lovers strolled hand in hand as if the world were entirely their own and they were absorbed in the magic of being in love.

People would congregate on the Common to listen to various speakers who expressed their opinions concerning everything from religion and abolition of slavery to the politics of the day, both local and national. Many concepts were expounded. Those who had nothing better to do stopped and listened.

The afternoons were alive with the sounds of bees. Roses had begun to bloom on fences and in the neatly kept gardens on Beacon Hill. The coaches had their tops down; people rode about in the open air, enjoying the movement of the vehicle as it created a circulation of cooler air. No doubt summer was well on its way.

Jane Augusta Ornby-Clark, round and jolly, bubbling with the excitement she usually expressed, moved along the streets. She had not exercised much during the winter. Getting back to the effort of walking always involved a breaking-in period for her. But she knew that after the first aches of muscular pain and cramps, she would have herself back into condition for taking those long, pleasurable strolls she enjoyed—particularly in the afternoon and early evening. The climb up Beacon Hill was enough to cause her to stop several times along the way to catch her breath. She used the time to glance about at the lovely houses, the lawns and well-trimmed hedges, the flowers. A stray cat wandered by and arched its back as she reached to pet it. Dogs and children seemed to like her, going out of their way to be recognized by her. She patted affection wherever it would be received and giggled in her usual jovial way. She liked life and all the changes of seasons. Happy-go-lucky and filled with a wonderful sense of being, she paraded farther up the hill as if it was quite by accident she was heading toward the home of her aunt, Patricia Phenwick.

Jane Augusta stopped again before she reached the house to blot her brow with a handkerchief Normally she would approach the ominous mansion in a carriage, but with the advent of summer only days away, she simply enjoyed the journey by foot.

Greeted at the door by Dietrich, she was shown into the foyer, which always had a cool yet pleasant atmosphere. She ran a hand about her gray hair as if to feel that each curl was in place and no straggly bits had blown loose.

Dietrich returned a few moments later to announce that Mrs. Phenwick would appreciate an audience with her niece. Jane Augusta thanked the butler. She took the stairs to the second floor with some effort. With the exception of Marcia, Jane Augusta was the female relative most devoted to the old lady. She had spent many hours with Patricia, both during good health and illness. She possessed no motivation other than to exude the expression of love she felt for Patricia Phenwick. But she expressed love to everyone she met, maintaining a very positive, loving attitude toward all. She vacillated from one philosophy to another and although she was a regular churchgoer, she had developed many thoughts regarding religion through her conversations with Patricia. It was always a challenge to encounter the old lady in dialogue. She looked forward to it; they both did.

Jane Augusta bubbled as she entered the room on the second floor wherein Patricia was propped up in bed. She had gathered a bouquet of daisies, which she gave to Ilene, suggesting that they be instantly put in water before they wilted.

"You're looking quite your old self today, Aunt Patricia," Jane Augusta said in her usual robust way. "Joseph tells me you are improving."

"Improving *what*?" Patricia asked.

"Improving your health. You're much more radiant today, I must admit, than I have seen you in a long time. Joseph says you have rallied for the better—that spring agrees with you."

"I don't know that anything agrees with me anymore," Patricia commented, "because I am disagreeable. It's kind of you to say so, Jane Augusta, to express your feelings, to come and visit an old lady. The daisies are lovely. I only wish I had the strength to go out and pluck my own bouquet. Those days are gone forever, I fear, at least in this lifetime."

"I saw my brother Ted off on the ship this morning. He will be in Europe most of the summer," Jane Augusta related. "I believe his mission is two fold. First to further his own education; second to permit his sons to handle his patients. Perhaps they will develop larger practices of their own while he's away. Ted doesn't need to work. He's certainly well enough off to live comfortably for the rest of his life. He likes dealing with people—and he enjoys learning. He's very interested in this subject of the working of the mind. I don't know any of the details. He tells me about it when he comes to visit; but even his wife, Louise, isn't able to comprehend all that he has to say. She, of course, remained in Boston. I will have to spend many hours with her because she gets to be such a lonely person at times."

"Dear Jane Augusta, the backbone of the Ornby family," Patricia commented. "What would they do without you?"

"They would get along quite well, I have no doubt," Jane Augusta said with a giggle. "It's just that big sister has looked after them all for so long. My brothers look up to me. My sisters—well, they've been away from Boston for a long time—those who lived. But I hear from them occasionally."

"What of you, Jane Augusta? Are you truly happy?" Patricia asked.

"I'm as happy as I expect to be," the middle-aged lady responded. "I'm certainly rarely sad, then only during moments of crisis or change." She looked with an understanding expression at her aunt.

"Crisis and change?" Patricia commented. "Isn't that what life is all about? Wouldn't it be dull if everything were the same every day, and we went about doing exactly the same thing for an entire lifetime? It would become a bore. As one grows old, life becomes a bore anyway, a monotonous routine. Had I not been absorbed all these months in relating the family history to Marcia, I would have become dismal and depressed, being confined in this solitary room. Now I must find a new project on which I can work."

"A new project, Aunt Patricia? Whatever can you be thinking?" Jane Augusta questioned, giggling uneasily as she sat in the chair opposite the old lady and studied the face that had once been so beautiful and was now lined with the wrinkles of time.

"I would go mad if I didn't have my little projects," Patricia commented. "I can no longer hold a pen so that my scribbles are legible. Nor do I have the poetic thoughts that hounded me during younger years. Still I do have a project in mind."

"For goodness' sake, what is it Aunt Patricia?"

"I wish to perform a little magic," the old lady explained with a wry smile.

"Magic? Oh, surely Aunt Patricia—"

"Oh, surely, Aunt Patricia *what*?" questioned Patricia. "Don't you think me capable of it?"

"It depends on what sort of magic you're intending to perform," Jane Augusta quickly said. "I have know you long enough to know that there is nothing impossible for you once you set your mind to it."

"Quite true—quite true," Patricia remarked. "An excellent observation. For that reason I have chosen a project which can be accomplished right from my bed. It requires no writing whatsoever."

"For goodness' sake, tell me about it, Aunt Patricia. You know you have my curiosity up."

"What would you say if I were to tell you that I was going to create a Phenwick woman?" Patricia asked, a distant smile touching her lips.

"Create a Phenwick woman? Oh, Aunt Patricia—how could you—you're far too old—that is—"

"I don't mean to create her from my womb, Jane Augusta. Do be serious." The old lady chuckled.

"Well, if a girl isn't born into the Phenwick family, the only way she could possibly become a Phenwick woman is to marry a Phenwick man," Jane Augusta argued.

"Yes, precisely."

"But—what Phenwick men are available?" Jane Augusta questioned, her eyes becoming round and her cheeks swelling with a puff of air.

"You seem to forget my nephew Gordon."

"The preacher?" Jane Augusta sounded incredulous. She gasped as if she had heard a most horrifying suggestion.

"He is a Phenwick man," Patricia said. "As erratic and bizarre as he appears to be, one cannot deny that Gordon is a Phenwick. As a Phenwick, his wife has every right to become a Phenwick woman."

"But every Phenwick man doesn't—I mean—look at Gus."

"Gus Phenwick?" questioned Patricia. "Poor Augustus was a family misfit."

"And you don't believe that Gordon is?" Jane

Augusta asked hastily. "I mean he certainly isn't like his brother. Nor like any of the other Phenwick men I know, who are devoted to business and the family interests. On the contrary, Gordon is quite a colossal bore with his religious tactics and extremism."

"I well know that, Jane Augusta," the old lady announced. "At this moment it is unimportant. That sweet girl who has gone to put those daisies in the water—and I will dismiss her for a brief recess while we continue to talk, should she return—is quite a wonder to me."

"I don't understand. Do you mean that Irish girl?"

"That Irish girl is Ilene Dumphy," Patricia stated. "A singular creature to say the least."

"She is a pretty thing, I have noticed," commented Jane Augusta. "Still what has she to do with your project?" Again she gasped as she began to perceive a slight inkling of her aunt's intentions. "You don't mean—?"

"Precisely. I believe you quite well comprehend what I have in mind, Jane Augusta."

"But she's nothing but a serving girl, an Irish immigrant."

"Do you mean to say you don't believe she is good enough to become a Phenwick woman?"

"Why should she? I mean—"

"You have heard the legend of Augusta choosing the potential heiresses to the title of Phenwick woman, haven't you?"

"I know there are superstitions," Jane Augusta stammered. "I've never smelled the violets, if that's what you mean."

"That's because you're not a Phenwick woman, my dear niece. You are in the lineage of Augusta, but you were not chosen to become a Phenwick woman. There is quite a distinction, I might add. Not that you're not a deeply beloved member of the family, because you are."

"I never aspired to obtain such a title. I'm a Phenwick twice removed—I believe that's the way you express it," Jane Augusta commented. "Do you mean to tell me this common serving girl has been given the scent of violets?"

"She has indeed," Patricia returned. "At least that is the conclusion I have reached. On several occasions she has made comment on it. I am certain from my quizzing of other members of the family that Ilene is unaware that this legend exists as to the choosing of the Phenwick women. Still it may only be coincidence."

"Of course it's coincidence, Aunt Patricia. She's hardly what I would call—"

The door opened and Ilene entered the room. The daisies were neatly arranged in a pretty little blue vase.

"B'gorra, 'twas a problem findin' a proper container for the flowers," Ilene stated as she set them on the table nearby so Patricia could admire them. "Aren't they lovely? I do believe they're the prettiest daisies I've seen all year."

"Ilene, why don't you take a recess for a while? Go down and fix yourself a cup of tea and have a cake or something," Patricia suggested.

"I can nay leave you alone, Mrs. Phenwick. 'Twould nay be proper."

"It will be quite proper. Jane Augusta will sit with me for a while. When she tires of it, I'll ring for Dietrich to fetch you back."

"Very well, Mrs. Phenwick," she said smiling sweetly as she turned to leave the room.

"She is a pretty thing," Jane Augusta remarked, "now that I look at her in a different light."

"She's beautiful. She has a fine carriage when she doesn't slouch. From all appearances she seems to be bright and intelligent—despite her superstitious fancies."

"Her superstitious fancies, Aunt Patricia?"

"As you have observed, she is Irish, and they do have their strange beliefs. She is forever doing little things like crossing her fingers when she wants something to be positive in her favor, or spitting on her palm and rubbing it on her backside. Although not a Catholic, she crosses herself as if calling on God when a slight thing goes wrong. Other little gestures too numerous to mention are indicative of a superstitious nature. But she believes such things ward off ills. If they work for her, they do so because she believes in them."

"I—I don't quite follow what your reasoning is, Aunt Patricia."

"My reasoning is that I need a project. What would be a better one than turning a—mere, as you observed—serving girl into a lady? There was someone in mythology who transformed an ordinary person into a lovely creature. The point is, with the proper education and encouragement, I believe any young lady can overcome the conditions of her birth and step up into the world. Take Marcia, for instance. As you recall, when my daughter Susannah found her she was nothing but a waif herself. Now look at her, my pride and joy, the grand lady of Edward House, one day to become the reigning matriarch of the family. Had Susannah not taken an interest in the girl and Marcia had been allowed to go her merry way, no doubt she would have become jaded by the experiences of living in the street and consorting with lower-class individuals. But she was resurrected from that kind of life. Now she has become an elegant lady, one with whom I am extremely pleased. Therefore, it strikes me that an appropriate project for me is to take this lovely Ilene and transform her into a magnificent creature. If I accomplish this I will have achieved the utmost of creativity—something poetic, romantic, and a final triumph for this life."

"I don't mean to be pessimistic, Aunt Patricia, but how do you intend to do such a thing?" asked Jane Augusta.

"I've already taught her to read aloud. She reads quite well and with expression. This she has learned in the past few weeks while she's been working for me. She writes my letters. She's become aware of her English. The next thing is to help her get rid of that Irish brogue, which is little by little being chipped away. Oh yes, she's going to be a fine image of a lady when I get through with her."

"And when you do get finished with her, Aunt Patricia?" Jane Augusta questioned. "What then? Turn her to the dogs?"

"Turn her to the dogs?"

"I mean create her into a masterpiece only to be abused by Gordon Phenwick?"

"I don't believe Gordon will abuse her too greatly," Patricia stated. "She could give Gordon the incentive to be a different man. I think one of his basic problems is that he has lost touch with reality, has become somewhat imbalanced by his fanaticism. If he could be persuaded to take a beautiful wife, who has worldly charm, he might be redeemed of his habits of proselytizing and evangelical raving."

"You put a great deal of stock in the power of one woman over a man, Aunt Patricia."

"If anyone can affect Gordon, I believe it will be Ilene. She's a very understanding, outgoing person. She herself is immersed enough in superstition and belief, albeit quite different from Gordon's, that she could adapt somewhat to his way of life *if* he will adapt somewhat to hers," Patricia said. "I think of Elias and myself."

"You're manipulating things, Aunt Patricia," Jane Augusta observed. "I can see where it might be possible to alter and improve upon Ilene—not that her beauty needs improving on—but to do so for the purpose of converting Gordon is a preposterous supposition."

"You may be right, Jane Augusta. Still I want to give it a try. Perhaps Ilene will never conquer Gordon, but before I die, I want to feel that I have accomplished the transformation of this girl into an elegant lady," Patricia declared. "If I cannot arrange for a suitable marriage into the family, then I shall see that she is properly introduced to a gentleman of society. There is an affinity between Marcia and Ilene, with which I am pleased. With the right encouragement, I have no doubt that Marcia will accept her as a peer, once Ilene is the accomplished lady I intend to make of her. Don't laugh at me, Jane Augusta, or shake your finger, because I have set my mind to this project. I will work on it until the end of my days, if need be."

CHAPTER NINE

During the long hours which she spent with Patricia Phenwick, Ilene Dumphy learned many lessons. She dilligently sought to improve her speech, gradually eliminating much of the heavy brogue she had possessed. Patricia often corrected words and the pronunciation of them, until, frustrated by the process of learning, Ilene began to have doubts about her ability to accomplish what Patricia wanted. However, Patricia was encouraging, as was Marcia, when the opportunity arose.

While the old lady napped at least twice during the day, Ilene perfected her skill at sewing. Marcia had given her several dresses which the girl could make over into attractive garments for herself. Adept with the needle, she created a wardrobe that was quite stunning and accentuated her comeliness. Many of the dresses she redesigned, making them over so that they were not recognizable as having been worn by her mentor. She was handy with whatever she put her mind to. While her fingers stitched out a hem or sewed a seam, her mind was constantly working on her lessons.

Patricia had made no promise directly to the girl. The ever-increasing awareness Ilene had of violets more and more convinced the old lady that she was right in what she was doing.

Ilene took supper with Patricia in her room, and they conversed over the finely prepared meal. Patricia's appetite was small whereas Ilene's was healthy. It was an occasion wherein Patricia could superintend the refinement of the girl's table manners, teach her which utensil to use and the proper way of holding it. When she made a mistake, Patricia was quick to correct her. Ilene sat straight-backed and learned the correct etiquette with remarkable speed. After supper Ilene would read aloud, doing her best to speak without an Irish accent. She had occasional mishaps with pronunciation, which Patricia let her know about. She rarely made the same mistake more than three times. She enjoyed the exercise of becoming mannerly or proper. Never had she been aware that she spoke differently from other people until Patricia had pointed out word by word where she erred.

At seven o'clock Stella Murphy appeared to take over her shift. By then the old lady had tired. With the exception of a brief conversation or perhaps an evening visitor she was ready to sleep early.

As soon as Ilene was dismissed on those warm summer evenings, she would go to her room and choose one of her lovely gowns suitable for strolling outside. Once she had decorated herself and looked quite a lady, she prepared to go for a stroll down Beacon Hill and wander toward the Common. She liked the evening conversations, the orations and the views expressed. With all the elegance she was obtaining, she was still an earthy person who wanted to keep in touch with those with whom she had been raised.

Eyes observed her as she moved gracefully down the hill, some from lawns, others from behind windows. Tongues whispered about her, speculating on the identity of the lovely creature who took the evening strolls and who fearlessly went out alone, not to return before night had invaded the sky along the lantern-lit streets.

"I don't know, Moorduke, what's happening to me," she said softly. "But I can tell a change is coming over me. Do you appreciate it? I'm glad that you do." The rustle of her skirts obscured her whispered words. The evening breeze came up from the harbor to blow gently against her face. "I'm very fond of Mrs. Phenwick. With all of her stern discipline, she's a fine lady—and one for whom I am proud to work. I'm glad that you like her too. She asks about you regularly and wonders what you're up to. I try to tell her that you're not really up to anything. I don't mean to offend you Moorduke."

As she approached the Common she said, "It is best that I don't converse too much with you in public. People will think I am talking to myself. We both know that is not the case, but complete strangers might take a different attitude—don't you think? I don't understand. Do I speak that differently now? Then I have improved, haven't I? I hope Mrs. Phenwick is pleased. You should be pleased for me too, Moorduke, because I'm lifting myself up, as Mrs. Phenwick would say. I'm improving. That is very important to her—and she has convinced me that it's equally as important to me."

Ilene sauntered toward an area in the park

where a group of people were clustered. "Why do I come out like this at night? There's a reason, I believe. Something within me is percolating. I feel a warmth of excitement and anticipation."

Ilene stopped and stared down at the image she perceived beside her. "What do you mean, Moorduke? I think you are impudent suggesting that I am out searching for a man. Of course I know it's nature, the way things should be, that a girl my age should become interested in finding herself a man. But do you really think that is my motive for taking these evening strolls? Oh, you are impudent! Yes, I well know young men congregate here of an evening. But they're not particularly men of class and distinction. They're simple men. I admit I do enjoy attracting their attention. How can you say I'm playing with fire? I've never had a close male friend. I do deeply admire Dr. Joseph Ornby. He is a fine man. Were it not for Sheila I would be delighted to—not pursue him, Moorduke, but to—well—become friendlier with him, to establish a better acquaintanceship—if you know what I mean."

A group of people had gathered around a man who was loudly shouting in oratorical fashion. There was much noise and clamor of response. Ilene went close to the crowd, who were so absorbed in the histrionics of the speaker they were hardly aware of her presence. When she got a better look, she realized the man standing on the bench and expounding his theories, was none other than her brother Tim. He was short man with distinguishing features, and Ilene had always considered him a bit handsome. He was far from being a person of outstanding physical characteristics. He was a revolutionary and zealous rabble-rouser, a champion of the poverty-stricken immigrants. It was his desire to band them together in some sort of organization wherein they would have power to better their circumstances. The Irish in particular needed to be recognized as individuals and be given work as men, not treated as if they were slaves. His words were biting. When he spoke with heated excitement, his language became rowdy and often unintelligible. But the emotion he exuded rallied others like himself into a unifying cause.

When Tim Dumphy had finished, he jumped down from the bench and, while others gathered around him asking questions, pushed his way through the crowd. He had always had an eye for a beautiful girl.

Tim eyed his sister, not recognizing her. The look he gave her was most insinuating.

"You needn't look at me in such a way, Tim Dumphy," Ilene said. "You are disrespectful."

"Disrespectful. What are you talkin' about, lass? 'Tis nay disrespect I show you. 'Tis only interest."

"Tim, don't you recognize me? I'm your sister?"

"B'gorra! Is it you, Ilene? I would have niver know ya. What's becum o' ya? You don't even talk like yerself, much less look like the same garl I knew as a child."

"I've changed, Tim. I'm learning to become a lady."

"Cooo. Prim an' proper, ain't ya? What is it, lass? You've taken up with a gent o' aristocratic airs, is that it?" Tim accused.

"Far from it," Ilene returned. "I'm still working for Mrs. Phenwick. She has taken the time to help me alter myself."

"Alter yerself for what?" Tim asked. "You're a Dumphy and you'll always be one. You must remember yer place and who you are garl, and where you're frum. That's the way it is."

"I don't always have to be the poor little girl who came over on the immigrant boat, do I, Tim?"

"You've got it in yer blood, and that's what you are."

"Don't scold me, Tim. I like being what I am now. I enjoy wearing pretty clothes and feeling important," Ilene said. "I have respect for myself. I simply want you to understand that."

Tim gazed at her, not hiding his contempt. "Very well, I can see what you are up to, lass. 'Tis none o' me business. Exceptin' you are me sister. As me sister, I take a certain pride in ya. If you becum a grand lady, how kin I accept you as one o' me own? How kin I say, 'Here I am tattered rabble-rouser, and there is she herself a hifalootin' lady o' aristocracy'?"

"I am no such a thing, Timothy Dumphy," she returned, doing her best to control the anger that was welling within. "I am still Ilene Dumphy. I have improved myself. I have had opportunity and I've taken advantage of it. As for being the sister of a rabble-rouser, you know I will always do what I can to help you. I can't agree that your tactics are always the best."

"Oh, 'tis criticism you're givin' me, is it? You've becum some sort o' authority on what tactics should be?" charged Tim.

"Don't be closed-minded, Tim, but be happy for me," Ilene pleaded. "I could become a street girl, or marry and spend a life in drudgery washing clothes and tending little brats, while my youth and beauty quickly deteriorate. As I am, by improving myself, I may have the opportunity to meet some gentleman who will lift me even higher in this world."

"Oooh, you do have grand ideas, don't you, lass? Aye, I've niver seen th' like! And what will your dear sister Sheila be doin' while you're such an elegant lady?" Tim sneered. "She's worked all her life, she has, like our dear departed mither—to see that all o' us have cum up and lived as best we could. Aye, 'tis true, it's been mostly potatoes and cabbage most o' our days, but one day we poor people will becum strong and make a place for ourselves—and grow rich."

"Then you'll become part of the aristocracy, too," Ilene bit. "Will you still be the vulgar, uncouth, unlearned man that you are today, Tim? If so, you may achieve fortune, but you will never become part of the elite society."

"Oooh, 'tis th' elite society, is it? Well, you do have an uppity way about ya," Tim scorned. "I can nay stand and talk to you like this all evenin'. We'll go sometime and have us a beer and chat. I'll change yer mind for ya."

"We'll have a chat someday, Tim," Ilene agreed. "but I don't want you to attempt to change me from what I am becoming now. I watch the words I say. I pronounce them as clearly as I can with out a brogue."

" 'Tis separatin' you from yer family, that's what it is," Tim scowled.

"Tim—I am separated. I've become my own person now," Ilene uttered softly, sincerely. "I can only ask that you be proud of me for my accomplishments."

Tim glared into his sister's face. "I will be goin'

103

now, Ilene. I have other things to say to th' poor
and destitute, workers who make little or nothin'
for their efforts and go home to snifflin' babes and
women who are in tatters—and make th' best o'
their way o' life. You'll excuse me, please."

Ilene observed as her brother wiggled his way
back through the crowd. Soon his voice was ringing above the chatter of the throng. He immediately got their attention. She walked away, wondering what effect her relationship to that man
would have on the stately ambitions with which
Patricia Phenwick had imbued her. Still she was a
proud person, she kept telling herself. No matter
what her background had been, she would aspire
to become something better.

As Ilene wandered about the Common, she hesitated or stopped at various places to listen to the
orators as they expounded theories about this,
that and the other thing. Twice she encountered
speeches dealing with religious matters that bor-
dered on being sermons. Singers, instrumentalists,
a concertina player and a guitarist, who roved
about and sang, placed their hats on the ground
to receive pennies that were tossed to them. She
thought of it as a kind of carnival, that conglom-
eration of people who gathered to perform and be
entertained. Yet she felt on the perimeter of the
crowd, not one of them—merely an observer. In
times gone by, when she was only a street urchin
herself, she had come to listen to the singers and
speakers. Then she considered herself one of the
mass, now no longer. She had changed. She liked
the change. She could observe but not participate,
for she knew there was another kind of life, and
that was the life she wanted.

A group of people were singing a rousing hymn

to the accompaniment of two horns and a tambourine. A large number of people had gathered around the speaker, who was leading the singing. Out of curiosity she moved closer to watch what was happening. A half-dozen persons had obviously been brought along for the purpose of leading and inspiring the others. These individuals had been converted to the fundamental Christian principles espoused by the leader of the aggregation.

As Ilene got closer and craned her neck for a better glimpse of the proceedings, she recognized the man in the center of the crowd as Gordon Phenwick. He carried a worn and well-used Bible, which he held aloft and shook vigorously as the hymn came to an end.

"Praise be the Lord!" Gordon shrieked.

The others repeated what he said.

"On this blessed night, I come before you with instructions from God Almighty through the intervention of the Holy Spirit," Gordon announced, "to preach His holy word and bring forth the sinners from their degradation and iniquity! I call you now to repent of your ways, Put aside your sinning and become reborn Christians in Jesus Christ! Jesus Christ—oh, hallelujah!—died for your sins in bloody torment upon the cross, and three days later was resurrected for the salvation of mankind. Oh, but you sinners! You who have groveled in the uttermost depths of sin and transgression, you are the ones I have come to save, to lift out of the filthy gutter and raise to heights of glory! You have but to confess Jesus Christ as your only living savior, and you will be redeemed from lives of utter servitude to the devil! Satan himself has moved among you, but, praise the

Lord, he has not touched me, nor will he ever! For I am His holy disciple—and Jesus Christ is my only salvation *now* and *always!*"

Someone yelled, "Hallelujah!" Another screamed, "Praise the Lord!" Cries of "Amen!" followed.

Ilene listened to the bombastic spouting of the man, whose face was etched with fury and whose zealous presentation was dramatic beyond belief. He appealed to the emotions of the listeners and dared them at last to come forward, to fall to their knees and beg for forgiveness, to be saved and reborn anew into the life of a newborn Christian.

Ilene found the display emotionally charged, and felt herself being tugged by Gordon's magnetic words. She sensed a reaction of non-resistance as she seemed to be physically drawn toward him. The crowd sang another hymn while various individuals went to their knees before the arrogant preacher. He put his hands on their heads and prayed for them. There was much crying, weeping for the sinful lives they had led and the promise of salvation that lay ahead through their conversion in faith.

Ilene watched for nearly half an hour as the group slowly dispersed and only a few of the "saved" were left with those who had come with the organization. It was a glorious moment for Gordon Phenwick as he raised his hands high and prayed loudly, beseeching God in heaven to accept these sinners into his congregation that they might err no more. Then his fiery glance turned to the pretty face of Ilene Dumphy illuminated by lamplight.

Moving past the kneeling people, the weeping

and the wailing ringing in his ears, Gordon stepped to where Ilene was standing.

"The others are going back to the mission with the converts," Gordon said, "where they will be given a Christian baptism and the hope of a new tomorrow. Will you join us, little lady? Will you come and be saved, confess your sins and embrace Jesus Christ as your personal savior?"

"Thank you, Reverend Phenwick," Ilene replied softly. "While I was moved by your delivery, I was only mildly impressed with what you had to say."

"Do I know you?"

"We have met."

"The face is familiar. Ah yes, you used to work for my aunt, didn't you?"

"I still work for her," Ilene assured him.

"I see. What brings you out into the Common this night?"

"A breath of fresh air, a stroll. After one sits with the old lady all day, a change is greatly needed," Ilene remarked.

"I can understand that only too well," Gordon said, deciding to change his tactics as his eyes investigated the figure of the attractive young lady. "Will you stroll with me for a while?"

"Aren't you going back to the mission with the others?"

"No. I have concluded my part in the service for today. There are others who will carry forth from here and aid the wretched sinners to find peace of mind in Jesus Christ at last," he stated piously.

"Where will we stroll?" Ilene asked, somehow fascinated and intrigued by the man.

"About the Common. I will put away my piety

for a while and just be an ordinary man, if it will put you at ease."

"I find that you are quite an attractive man," Ilene stated. "I have always been partial to men who are huskily built. Perhaps that is the Irish in me. Our men are often broad-shouldered and possessed with strong tempers."

"Do you think I have a temper, Miss—I don't recall your name."

"It is Ilene Dumphy," she said. "I believe you appear to have a temper."

"It's part of my work," Gordon explained. "When I am preaching the gospel, I become excitable and want to proclaim my enthusiasm to everyone within earshot. My temper rises when I witness the work of Satan, and how it is pulling mankind down into the depths of deprivation."

"Who is Satan?" Ilene asked innocently.

"You're Irish. Were you not raised a Catholic?" Gordon questioned.

"No. I am unchurched. My father is a descendant of the Orangemen, an Anglican. My mother was Catholic. We were raised in neither church because of the disputes between my parents over religious beliefs."

"Oh, you poor neglected soul," Gordon exclaimed. "I pity you. Your own salvation is desperately in need of reckoning with."

"I would rather not speak of such things, if you don't mind, Reverend Phenwick. I find it pleasant walking with you, but I prefer not discussing such matters at this time—if you please."

"Very well. I will condescend to put my churchly ways aside for the time being, although I can never be unaware of my Christian beliefs. Oh, when I think of that bloody death on Golgotha! When I ponder how He died to save us, it moves me!"

"Please, Reverend Phenwick, you said you would not," Ilene stated. "If you persist in doing so, I will have to excuse myself."

"No, no, I will resist the temptation to preach for the moment." Gordon smiled and presented a friendly expression as they stopped momentarily beneath the lamplight. "Aren't you afraid being out this time of the night in such a public place?"

"I never have been," Ilene returned. "I've come here since I was a girl. My brother is yonder, speaking to a crowd of people who are in desperate financial straits. He is an organizer."

"Ah, I appreciate the zeal of the park orators," Gordon commented. "There is something interesting in observing what goes on here, even with those who come to me, who are attracted to the hymns and the horns and tambourine. I often have tried to analyze why people mill about the Common of an evening. I have reached the conclusion that it is due to loneliness—desperate loneliness. These are people who are alone among their own kind. Many are derelicts, wasted souls who have nothing. Nothing physical, nothing mental, nothing spiritual. Without things of the spirit, every man is truly starved. We are first and foremost spirit. It was spirit that found our bodies in the first place, and it will be the spirit that goes on after we have discarded this flesh. Yet it is the contamination of the flesh that corrupts the spirit. You see across the way a wooden church. That is where I am preacher. It's an old building. One day we hope to build a new edifice for the glorification of Jesus Christ. At this time, we are desperately in need of funds, even to survive with the work we are doing. So we make do with an old church and pray that God Almighty will one day see fit to give us a glorious edifice in which we can worship Him and sing praises to His glory. Hallelujah!"

"I have noticed that church," Ilene acknowledged. "I'm familiar with the sight of it. But I freely admit I've never been inside. Nor, for that matter, have I ever been inside any church. They're unfamiliar to me."

"I—I still have my Bible," Gordon stated, "which I should like to return to the church. It will only take a few minutes. Would you care to join me and get a view of the interior of the house of God?"

"I don't know."

"You should come in and see what it is like," Gordon coaxed. "I will light the candles for you and present the altar with the cross hanging above it, and the pulpit. You can see for yourself what it is like."

"I don't believe I should take the time. It is getting late and I should be getting back to Edward House," Ilene said.

"I'll tell you what," Gordon returned. "If you will take just a few minutes with me to come inside, then I will see that you are walked back to Edward House. In fact I will personally do it. It is a great honor for me to enter into God's house, and you will honor me by accepting my invitation now."

Gordon reached to take her arm and gently guided her toward the church.

"Something comes to mind that is perplexing, Reverend Phenwick," Ilene remarked.

"What is that?"

"You are a member of the wealthy Phenwick family, are you not?"

"Of course."

"Do you have wealth of your own?"

"A reasonable amount. Why do you ask?"

"I was wondering why you did not put money into the church."

"I do give significant money to the church. I tithe, giving ten percent of what I receive."

"And ten percent of what you own?"

Gordon fumbled a moment trying to find a word. He could not. He coughed and cleared his throat. "The preacher does not support the church financially. It is the privilege of the many who come, the members of the flock, to provide funds for the running of the church."

"Oh. I was just wondering. It was a curiosity to me, that is all."

"Come along, my child," Gordon stated. He applied pressure to her arm as he pushed her toward the church.

CHAPTER TEN

A weatherworn sign on the side of the building read: "Welcome all ye that enter here—confess your sins and I will give you peace." Ilene observed it as they approached the cold, wooden building that appeared as if its better days were behind it. The ominous dark exterior was foreboding.

Gordon put a large key into the front-door lock. There was a rusty sound when it was turned. The interior was black. A stale odor came from within that was far from pleasant.

Seeing that Ilene appeared hesitant, he said, "I will go in first and light a few candles that you may see the way."

Her impulse in that moment of being left alone was to escape, not to enter. But she possessed a natural curiosity. She had come that far. If the church was truly a place of God, why would Ilene have anything to fear? She knew so little about religion, certainly nothing about the brand of it that Gordon Phenwick preached. Still her mother had always spoken with deep respect concerning her religious feelings.

Gordon emerged from the darkness like a looming creature. The candle in his hand illuminated his features, creating an almost diabolical expression. His large eyebrows were dark shadows going from the center of his face in an upward sweep toward his temples. His smile, in that light, was almost menacing, as was the piercing look in his eyes.

"This way, Ilene Dumphy," Gordon instructed. "Enter the house of the Lord."

Gordon put the key into the lock and turned it. Then he dropped the key into his pocket.

"Why did you do that?" questioned Ilene.

"Vandals." Gordon's voice was heavy with insinuation. "Tramps, derelicts creep in here at night to find a place to sleep. To avoid such an invasion, I keep the door locked—especially at night. There is the mission near the waterfront for those who have no place to go."

Ilene appeared to be satisfied with his explanation. Still she could not help but feel apprehensive as they moved through the dark foyer and into the main assembly room.

The chairs were not in regular lines, as if they had not been replaced into symmetrical rows after a meeting. In the flickering candlelight at the rear of the room Ilene could see a platform, a lectern and an oblong table against the far wall that was used as an altar. Two candles stood on the altar; two others were on the lectern; two more trembled flame opposite the lectern. With the one in Gordon's hand, there were seven candles lit. The tall windows were covered, probably with paint, to keep out daylight. The heat of the day was trapped in the building and the lack of ventilation created an uncomfortable atmosphere.

"This is where we hold our regular services," Gordon explained. Mounting the platform, he held his candle before the cross suspended

113

directly above the center of the altar. "We do not put on a lot of pretense and show. The cross and candles are our only symbols. Unlike the Catholics, we do not have statues, nor is the figure of Jesus Christ on the cross. He has been resurrected. Come closer and examine the cross, Ilene. It has a very emotional effect upon me and all true believers."

"I can see it perfectly well from where I am standing."

"I often kneel before the altar to pray for guidance from the Almighty," Gordon related. "Jesus Christ is my life. I weep when I consider the agony He endured for my salvation. Still there are times—no, I cannot say that." He glared at the girl, a look of anguish coming to his eyes. "I pray to be protected against the vile workings of Satan!"

Tiny prickles of anxiety began to move over Ilene and a strange taste came to her mouth. She swallowed hard. "I do not know of Satan."

"The evildoer! The malevolent force of the universe!" Gordon suddenly yelled. "He has power. Great power to tempt even the righteous into submitting to his desires. He is ever present waiting to pounce upon the likes of you. Unchurched! What a terrible thing to say!"

"It is true, Reverend Phenwick," Ilene stated. "I think it time we went."

"First, you must join me in prayer," Gordon beseeched. "We must pray for your soul—and for mine."

An even stranger sense of apprehension came over Ilene. Her back was alive with the prickly sensation. Her hands and lips trembled and a terrible urgency to leave that place presented itself.

Her palms moist, her vision distorted with un-known fear, she felt held to one spot, unable to move. "Pray—pray for *your* soul?"

Gordon stared up at the cross, then turned for-ward, bent slightly and put his arms up before his forehead as if attempting to shield himself from some danger. The Bible fell from his hand. Ilene feared that he would also drop the candle, as it was tilted to the side and wax dripped to the floor. What weird transformation was coming over the man?

When Gordon lowered the protecting arm be-hind which he had been hiding, his face appeared distorted. His eyes were wild and appeared al-most red, reflecting a glassy passion. Sneering with his mouth open and his teeth clenched tightly together, he looked grotesque in that eerie candlelight.

"Yes, you must pray for me," Gordon stormed. "I am mortal, therefore periodically set upon by the devil." He wiped his mouth with the back of his hand but the dreadful sneer would not go away.

Ilene cringed and managed to step backward. "What is wrong with you?" she questioned.

"The devil brings forth my carnal nature," Gor-don announced. "I, too, am flesh and passion! My lust for earthly pleasures is ignited by the fury of Satan. He makes me do vile acts. Oh, I pray, screeching for Satan to get behind me—to get away. But he persists as if he gets inside my skin and taunts me to express my human characteris-tics, to seek satisfaction for nagging desires."

"I don't know how to pray," Ilene whimpered.

"It is too late for that now," Gordon hollered. "Ilene Dumphy, you have been brought here tonight to fulfill my needs. I knew that the instant I saw you standing in the Common. While I believed at first that I sought your salvation, Lucifer whispered in my ear and aroused me with lustful passions that could only be relieved by conquering your body."

"I thought you were a man of God," Ilene said, trembling so that she was barely able to speak.

"Basically I am a man of God," Gordon declared, putting the candle he was carrying in a holder, "but there are times when I cannot withstand the temptation of Lucifer! I do not have the endurance that Jesus Christ had in the wilderness when He was tempted by that force of evil." He lunged toward her.

Ilene drew back, managing to get a chair between herself and the leering man. "I'll be goin' now."

"No, no, Ilene Dumphy," Gordon yelled, "you will stay and submit to my will. I hold the key to your salvation and you must permit me to glorify you."

"I know what you're after, Reverend Phenwick," Ilene returned, "and 'tis nay me desire—I mean it is not my desire—to be accosted by you. I am a lady—or at least I'm working on it. You will not have your way with me!"

"Resistance from a child of the gutter?" Gordon exclaimed, then laughed menacingly. "Your brother is a common rabble-rouser and an abuser of innocent woman. I know what he is and the terrible things he does."

"My brother's life is his own," Ilene charged. "It is no reflection on me."

"But it is! You are shanty Irish. No matter what finery Patricia Phenwick dresses you in, nor how she persuades you to refine your speech, you are still from the lowest of the low," Gordon declared. "Your body is made for the pleasure of man!"

"It is not!" she said defiantly. "No man has ever touched me, nor will he until I am properly married. That is a promise I made to my mother in her dying days. It is a sacred oath."

Gordon pushed the chair aside and reached out for her.

Quickly Ilenē maneuvered to another chair, picking it up. He grabbed it from her hands and flung it aside.

"Satan says I must take what I want!" Gordon proclaimed. "And I will do so!"

Ilene caught hold of still another chair, swinging it as she lifted it. The leg hit against Gordon's face.

Momentarily stunned, Gordon reeled backward. Ilene dropped the chair and ran toward the front of the hall. Gordon was immediately behind her, reaching out several times before he connected with her skirt. The next moment she was on the floor, sprawled face down.

Gordon stood above her. "Repent to Satan, you tramp of the gutter!"

As he straddled her and began to drop to his knees, Ilene kicked wildly, yet aiming her foot at a vulnerable spot. The impact of her foot was painful to Gordon who grabbed himself and staggered backward with agonizing torment.

Ilene scampered to her feet and ran to the front door. It was locked. She panicked, looking for another means of escape.

Short, stubby fingers connected with her shoulders. She was propelled away from the door, back against the wall that separated the foyer from the main assembly hall. Gordon lurched forward in the near darkness. By inches Ilene managed to elude him, spinning about. Gordon crashed into the wall and groaned.

Seizing the opportunity, Ilene ran back into the assembly hall, where there was enough light to guide her to a door.

Gordon using ungodly words, grumbled angrily. Moments later his footsteps were clomping over the wooden floor. "There is no escape for you, wench!"

Ilene tugged at the door. It came open. She entered darkness, and bumped her leg against an unseen object. Reaching her hands about, she searched to find the way. She had entered a small room. Her hands touched a desk. She turned to run into a small bed, perhaps only a cot. Going farther, she felt bookshelves and volumes in a disorderly arrangement upon them.

The candlelight appeared in the doorway, illuminating the terrible expression of revenge on Gordon Phenwick's face. He slammed the door shut and pulled the bolt on it. Panting, he tore at his cravat and the buttons on his vest. He had removed his coat en route to that small room.

"So Satan has led you to my private chamber, has he?" Gordon gloated.

Ilene cowered against the bookshelf as she watched Gordon put the candle holder on the desk and remove his vest. As he placed his vest on the chair beside the desk, Ilene heard a muffled clunk. She recalled that he had put the front-door key in his vest pocket.

Gordon removed his boots, all the while staring at her with a menacing expression. "The will of

Satan must be fulfilled! But no gentleman takes his pleasure fully clothed, does he, Ilene?"

"I wouldn't know about such things," she replied. "Oh, Moorduke, where are you when I need you most?"

Gordon's shirt was flung onto the desk. "Cry out all you like. Even God Almighty cannot help you now, not until Satan has had his way." He tugged at his trousers. "You must understand, Ilene, that this is not my doing, but the work of Satan. He must express himself through me. If I do not allow him to have his way occasionally, he interferes with my task of saving wretched sinners."

"But he is making a sinner of you!" Ilene muttered.

"Even so, I will later repent and be forgiven by the grace of Jesus Christ," Gordon said, standing only in his underclothing. "There are times when I am completely unable to resist the prodding of the devil. He is a powerful force, second only to God. The two wrestle within me. But when the devil fills me with such an overpowering lust as I have now, there is no intervention until that urge has been satisfied. I will spend the night in prayer because of this. Please try to comprehend what a terrible ordeal I am experiencing."

At that moment Ilene realized she was dealing with a very disturbed and tormented man. Her hand connected with a book. But how many volumes could she fling at him before he overcame the onslaught and wrenched her wrist until she was supine upon that cot? She was confronting an animal, not a man. What had Patricia said about the double side of his mother's nature? Good and evil all in one person? If Ilene could

119

only think, but her senses were distorted by the looming danger before her.

Gordon was unfastening buttons when he became startled by a small light that began to glow on the bookshelf next to Ilene. He stopped before his chest was fully exposed. "Oh my God! Fire!"

"Fire?" Ilene turned her head to the side to see where his eyes were focusing. "Thank goodness, Moorduke, you've come at last. I'd given you up."

"'Tis a fine position I've found ye in," a tiny voice seemed to say. "Ye've interrupted me from a long and peaceful nap, ye have."

Gordon rubbed a hand across his eyes. His fingers went back to find the buttons that had just been unfastened. "It's my imagination!"

"No. 'Tis nay yer imagination, Mr. Holier-than-thou," the voice piped up. "Would ye like to see more o' me? 'Tis a bit o' magic I kin do." The figure of the little person grew to at least twelve inches.

"Lucifer! What have you done to me?" Gordon cried.

"Can he see you, Moorduke?"

"Aye, occasionally I let meself be seen by others, but nay without good reason. With all his pretended holiness, the man is an agent o' Satan. I believe that is the expression he used."

"Who are you?" Gordon questioned. "I don't believe my eyes."

"Ye'll believe more than your eyes if I grow another five feet in front o' ya, won't ya?"

"You can't! You're an illusion!" Gordon declared.

"If that be the case, that I'm an illusion, then I kin well grow to ten feet tall, kin't I?"

"What do you want of me?" Gordon gasped.

120

"I want ye to pull back on yer britches, I do. 'Tis bad enough to expose yerself to a garl, much less to a fancy lady, but 'tis quite another to show yerself in a state o' complete undress to a leprechaun."

"You're an incubus!" Gordon stated. "I am not the only one tormented by the devil."

"Incubus, is it? Well now, I nay would be too sure o' that. But I suspect ye've bin set upon by a succubus or two—if ye believe in that sort o' thin', which I don't."

"And I don't believe in leprechauns!" Gordon declared, regaining some of his composure.

"Ye don't, don't ye? Well now—"

The figure beside the bookshelf expanded until it appeared to be of human proportions.

"My God! It can't be happening!" Gordon screamed.

"Ye see lass, this man is full o' hooey, and tryin' to fill ye with m'larky. 'Tis the truth, is it nay, Reverend Phenwick?"

Gordon was trembling with such fear that he fell onto the floor in a prone position and began beating his fists against it. "Oh, God in heaven, forgive me! Jesus Christ, come and comfort me in this hour of my agony! I don't know what demon this is that has come after me, but I repent! I repent!"

"I've used enough o' me energy for one night," the image beside Ilene said. "I'm liable to drive the man insane if I persist. It would be a short drive at that."

Gordon was blubbering, jabbering incoherently.

Ilene stepped around him and went to the door. She had the bolt out of it's position before she remembered to get the key from Gordon's vest pocket.

Gordon was tossing about on the floor, jerking spastically as if he were having a convulsion.

Ilene glanced back into the room. "Moorduke? Where did you go, Moorduke?"

Gordon jerked upward as if he were attempting to rise from the floor. Ilene quickly went through the door and closed it behind her. Then she made her way as fast as possible to the front door. Her hands trembled as she attempted to insert the key into its hole.

Finally she was out into the night air. The key was left in the lock. She ran from the ominous building and up the street. Without looking back, she hurried until she was well out of the vicinity of the church. She did not recall the journey back to Edward House. Her panic did not cease until she was safely in her room on the third floor.

CHAPTER ELEVEN

Stuart had had business to attend to that evening. Marcia remained home to work on her writing. The old house was quiet, but well ventilated; the night wind rattled objects and created a kind of eerie sound. But Marcia liked to have the windows open and an abundance of fresh summer air. Had Ilene been home, Marcia would have persuaded the girl to accompany her for a stroll about the gardens. Ilene was good company.

If Marcia had thought of it earlier, she would have put the writing aside and gone to visit Nancy and the children. But she had not. So she would sit and listen to the wind whistle through, rattling things as it went. Sweet fragrances were in the air, along with the night sounds of crickets, peepers and other nocturnal creatures. Periodically an owl would call and an answer would come from a different direction.

Marcia was startled when she heard the hurried racing of footsteps up the stairs. They did not have the sound of her husband's. Then when they dashed up to the third floor, she was convinced they belonged to one of the servants. It was the urgent tone of the anxious steps that roused her suspicion. She would go investigate.

By the time Marcia reached Ilene's room, the

girl had pulled ot of her torn dress and was about to remove her underthings. Ilene had been crying, her eyes red and trails of tears streaking down her face.

"What is it, Ilene?" Marcia inquired. "I've never seen you in such a state."

"Oh, Miss Marcia!" The girl ran to the other and hugged her tightly. "I had a terrible experience."

"Do you wish to tell me about it?"

"No, I don't," Ilene returned. "It was too frightening."

Marcia soothed her, stroking her hair as Ilene burst into full sobbing. "Let the tears come, Ilene. Let them wash the torment away from your mind."

Ilene cried for nearly five minutes while she clung to the young woman. The nearness of a warm, understanding human being was comforting and she needed that release of emotions.

"I was accosted by a man," Ilene said and burst again into tears.

"A man? Did he harm you?"

"He tried—he tried to have his way with me," Ilene cried. "But I managed to get away from him in the end."

"Who was this man? Did you know him?" Marcia asked.

Ilene blinked a startled expression, fear twisting in the corners of her face. "No. No, I didn't." She had her fingers crossed. "'Twas dark and he pounced upon me from out of the shadows. He tore my clothing. My beautiful dress is ruined. I'll never be able to mend it."

"How did you manage to get away from him?"

Marcia persisted. "Did someone come to your rescue?"

"Yes—and no. I mean—well, I'm afraid you wouldn't understand, Miss Marcia," Ilene said.

"I will try to."

"It—well—it was Moorduke," Ilene explained. "He not only made himself visible, but he expanded himself to mortal size. I was fair alarmed myself to see him do such a thing. If it was all an illusion, the man saw it too. I don't rightly see how we could both have the same hallucination."

"That's a preposterous story, Ilene," Marcia remarked as she tried to lighten her words with laughter.

"I know it is. And I don't fully believe it meself—I mean myself. The only thing I can figure is that the man was as superstitious as I am."

Marcia finally eased herself from the girl's tenacious grip and went to get a cool wet cloth to wash the pretty Irish face. It was a lovely gesture of friendship and understanding, greatly appreciated by Ilene.

"Why don't you put on another dress and come down and sit with me in my room?" Marcia asked. "There's a nice ocean breeze down there. Stuart will be late and I would very much like to have some company. You're certain the man did not go all the way with you or harm you in any way so that you need attention?"

"No. He was more interested in getting out of his own clothes," Ilene stated, "than he seemed to be about getting me out of my own."

"An exhibitionist. Such terrible men can be frightening, I've heard. Fortunately I've never encountered such an individual, although I once came very close to having a devastating experience. My brother Gregory, Jim Cornhill—who is now my stepfather—Stuart and Gordon came to my rescue."

"Gordon?" Ilene questioned, a whimper in her voice.

Marcia stared at the girl, but could not decipher the expression. She chuckled. "That was before he was such a zealous preacher—Gordon, I mean. He was on his way toward it, but he was still a boy at the time. As a matter of fact, Gordon was captured and the antagonizers were going to strip him and leave him alone in an old abandoned warehouse on the docks. I felt sorry for him then. I suppose, because of that incident, I have tried to keep an open mind about my brother-in-law and have attempted to understand his peculiar ways. I mentioned the situation once to Joseph and Dr. Ted, but they say they believe Gordon was headed in his singular direction long before that happened."

"Was he only a boy?"

"In his late teens, I believe," Marcia responded. "I never knew his mother—nor his father very well. Nancy tells me that Lillian Phenwick was herself a queer person. She was as strongly religious as Gordon—no doubt he gets it from her—but she was also involved with some of the black arts."

"The black arts?" questioned Ilene, now going to find a dress into which she could change.

"I believe Nancy said it was voodoo," Marcia said. "It was some kind of Satan worship, I suppose. She had two sides to her nature: an overzealous Christian persuasion, and, apparently, just the opposite. She believed in both the power of God and the power of Satan. Nancy related that she found waxen likenesses of herself from time to time—and that she endured terrible physical stress until she was bedridden because of that voodoo power. You see, Lillian had never been accepted as a Phenwick woman, and she was jealous of every other woman who was—and any who had the potential of being one. It affected her mind. Obviously she was quite insane before she died in a horrible fire. Jane Augusta was there; she told me about it."

"The poor woman," Ilene observed, tying a sash about her waist. "Then we must have pity for poor Reverend Phenwick, mustn't we? That Mrs. Phenwick's illness didn't affect—? I mean—"

"Stuart?" asked Marcia. "No, thank God, he seems perfectly normal and sane. Perhaps I'm prejudiced by love, but I sincerely believe—because he rejected his mother's beliefs—that he was saved from a terrible fate. I'm not as certain about Gordon. Come along. We'll continue our talk in my room."

"It is much nicer down here," Ilene said a few minutes later as she settled into a comfortable chair by the window.

"Shall I ring and have Nora bring us some tea?" Marcia asked.

"Oh no, it is too warm for anything hot."

Ilene settled deeply into the chair. Marcia watched her, noting the still troubled look that periodically twitched a her face.

"About this man who attacked you—?" Marcia commented.

Again Ilene crossed her fingers beneath the folds of her dress. "It was dark. I did not get a good look at him. I wouldn't know him if I were to see him again. I would rather not speak of him."

"Perhaps it is best to put the entire incident as far from your mind as you can," Marcia stated, "and as quickly as possible."

"I saw me—my brother this evening in the Common," Ilene said, to change the subject. "He did not recognize me at first. Then he got into a terrible temper when he discovered I'd improved my way of speaking and that I was bettering myself. He said I was getting uppity. Poor Tim, he's a rabble-rouser. The lad has a natural ability for leadership. It concerns me that he embraces peculiar causes. Oh, he has some very rowdy ideas. Revolutionary."

"Revolutionary? Oh dear, I don't like to hear that," Marcia remarked. "There is already so much talk about the slavery situation causing such strife in this country. Some say it will ultimately lead to war. I do hope not. Stuart is concerned. He says the situation between North and South has already put a tremendous stress on business conditions. Medallion has an office in Savannah, you know. Prentise Phenwick is in charge of it. Stuart has gone several times to speak with his Uncle Prentise, but there seems to be an insoluble condition arising. My husband always returns from such encounters with Prentise in a depressed state. Prentise has become a Southerner in his thinking and has become an anti-abolitionist. You will discover there is a stubborn streak in the Phenwicks."

"I've noticed that with Mrs. Phenwick," Ilene commented.

"And she isn't of a direct blood strain," Marcia related. "She only married into the Phenwick family. Her first husband had been adopted by Augusta Phenwick. Her second husband was the illegitimate child of Augusta's only son who lived to adulthood. Her daughter Rebecca has Augusta's blood, not her daughter Susannah. Ironically Susannah has the fieriness that would have pleased Augusta, whereas Rebecca is sedate and retiring. My husband, Stuart, is of the direct lineage of Augusta. Perhaps that explains some of his determined ways."

"They sound like a very complicated clan."

"What family isn't?" Marcia returned. She turned and looked away.

"What is it, Miss Marcia? Is something disturbing you?"

"Just speaking of my mother, Susannah," Marcia explained, "made me wish that she could be with me during my pregnancy. I would like her to be here when my baby is born. But England is a long way from Boston. In the last letter I received, she was planning to embark on another concert tour. That is her life and she loves it. I would be selfish to want her with me when her heart is in Europe. Perhaps in the fall, when the tour is concluded."

"I didn't know your mother played concerts."

"She's a pianist," Marcia said. "But I think time is catching up with her. Susannah said her critics were not as kind as they used to be. They still admire her skill, but they make references to her age."

"You must have been born late in her life."

"I was—but Susannah is not my mother—only my adopted mother. My real mother died when Gregory and I were children. Gregory lives in England with Susannah. He and Uncle Joshua manage the Medallion company there. Oh, I do miss Gregory, too."

"I suppose he is married and has a fine family," Ilene stated.

"Gregory is younger than I. He's quite a man about London. He has fit well into Susannah's way of life and Joanna's."

"Joanna?"

"She is my husband's aunt. His father's only sister. She's an actress and quite a marvelous person."

"Do you miss England?"

Marcia stared into the distance, not really focusing on anything. "Sometimes I wonder, Ilene. I miss Gregory, of course, and Susannah. And I greatly admire Joanna, Uncle Joshua and his wife, Olivia—but I don't know that I long to return. I love Boston because I've made a place for myself here. And my dearest Stuart is here."

"I admire the love you share with your husband," Ilene commented. "He is such a fine man, not like—I mean—"

"Not like whom, Ilene?"

"Not like so many other men," Ilene quickly replied. "One day I hope to find a man as nice as your husband."

"I pray you do, too—as long as he's *not* my husband."

"Oh, Miss Marcia!"

"I didn't mean anything by that, Ilene," Marcia said with a light laugh. "When I think of the years I put Stuart off and would not consent to marry him while I enjoyed the friendship of other eligible young Bostonians—oh, it makes me realize what a foolish person I was. But if I had not had the experience with other men, perhaps I would never have come to appreciate Stuart as I do. Our love is greater than I ever anticipated it might be."

Ilene stayed to chat a while longer. Soon sleep began to come and she became groggy. She caught herself about to doze off.

"'Tis best for me to go to my own room now, Miss Marcia," Ilene suggested. "My eyelids will not stay open."

"Thank you for sitting with me as long as you have, Ilene. I hope we can visit like this again on evenings when Stuart has to be away."

Ilene reached her room a few minutes later. Fatigue had completely filled her body. It was all she could do to remove her garments. Then, blowing out the lamp, she got into bed and stared up at the dark ceiling.

"Moorduke, I just wanted to thank you," she whispered. "I would never be able to sleep this night if that man had had his way. And goodness knows what all else he might have done to me. Maybe 'twould be best if I were to have a wee talk with Dr. Joseph. He would keep it our secret. Goodnight, Moorduke."

She soon fell soundly asleep.

CHAPTER TWELVE

Marcia greeted Dr. Joseph as he arrived the next day to examine Patricia. She made the suggestion that Ilene might require his counseling. Nothing serious. The night before she had seemed distraught and peculiar. Fortunately Joseph had a light day ahead. Marcia gave him few details in hopes that Ilene would unburden herself to him more than she did to her.

While examining Patricia, Joseph sent Ilene from the room, expressing that he would desire a cup of tea. The old lady's sharp senses perceived he was up to something. He examined Patricia maintaining his usual congenial, pleasant bedside manner.

When the examination was completed, Joseph remarked that he had few patients scheduled that day. He wondered if he might have Patricia's permission to take Ilene for a drive in the country.

Patricia surveyed her nice-looking, broad-shouldered nephew. His round features and body were not unattractive. True, he was not the handsome man that Stuart was, nor many of the young men she had known throughout the years; still he was not disagreeable to behold and possessed very sensual features. She gave permission.

Arrangements were made for Marcia to sit with

Patricia. Joseph made three other necessary calls and returned within an hour to meet Ilene, who was ready and waiting. The cook had prepared a picnic basket. It was decided that they would drive out into the country and stop in a convenient place to rest in the shade.

For some reason Ilene felt she must speak of her brother Tim and his ideas, as revolutionary as they were. While Joseph was not completely in sympathy with such thoughts, he could understand how persons of poor means would band together to obtain strength in hopes of altering their circumstances. He long had sympathathized with the imigrants and their poverty. He emphatically believed that the principal reason for their dire situation was not so much the moving to a new land but the relocation from rural to urban environments. In the city there was no land for farming. It was an entirely different way of life for these peasants who had existed contentedly close to the soil. Joseph confessed that he had had many long chats with Shelia on the matter of their financial condition; and Ilene's sister had discussed her concern about Tim on several occasions.

"Poverty can make a person become fanatical in his ways," Joseph commented as they drove along in the open shay, heading down the road toward Lexington.

Not only poor people become fanatical," remarked Ilene.

"Meaning?"

"I refer to Reverend Phenwick," Ilene mentioned, glancing slyly as if covering a nervous reaction.

"I've often wondered if Gordon's fanaticism is

hereditary or environmental. That is, if he got the tendency to be so from his mother or if he simply became aware of the conditions around him. I do not believe that Gordon is insincere in his beliefs."

"Maybe not insincere," Ilene said, "but he does have a strange two ways about him

"Two ways?"

"I think the word is 'hypocrite.' "

"Why do you say that, Ilene?"

"That's the way he strikes me, she returned, hiding her face again, hoping not to betray the images that were flashing into her mind from the night before. "My brother Tim, with all of his energy and determination, is only one way. He believes in the cause of his fellow men, those who are products of poverty. He acts accordingly, never deviating, never taking the side of the wealthy and the successful."

"I see what you mean. What does that have to do with Gordon?"

"The fact that Reverend Phenwick *is* from wealth," Ilene stated, "even dressing well while standing among the poor who gather about to listen and be converted—I don't know what it is. I get the feeling that he is saying one thing and being another. Do you understand what I mean?"

"No more so than with myself," Joseph commented. "I come from the same wealthy family, yet I certainly do not limit my medical practice to the opulent society. Rather I prefer working with those who are less fortunate. That is simply perpetuating my belief in the principle of giving and receiving. I believe that, by helping those less fortunate, I am helping myself toward a higher spiritual obtainment—as strange as that may seem.

Doing good unto others. I would like to believe that is what motivates Gordon."

"I cannot understand how a person can speak of God and Satan with honest belief in each," Ilene said.

"Gordon believes there are two powerful forces in the world," Joseph explained, "good and evil. To my way of thinking the whole allegory of the story of creation in the book of Genesis has to do with man's awareness that two such forces exist. If you recall the story of Adam and Eve, they ate fruit from the tree of *knowledge* of good and evil. They simply did not know evil existed—only good—until they had knowledge of it. It is like a stick, a line going in either direction toward infinity. At one end is good, the other end evil. They are both part of the same thing. Along that line there are degrees of good and evil, but there is only one line. Therefore, I cannot help but think that one line is what we call God or the principle of creativity and life. We simply approach it at whatever point on that line we are capable of so doing."

"I don't quite understand you."

"God and evil, God and Satan, whatever, are two opposing ends of the same thing," Joseph said.

"In that case, although I don't fully understand what you're talking about, Dr. Joseph, a person could interpret good and evil according to his own point of view."

"Basically that is the case. But we must realize that that is a distorted view," Joseph continued, "because wherever a person is at the time he is viewing whatever he is viewing may be affected by the state of his mind, by his awareness to reality. Then there are those who bounce from one end of the line to the other, who go from good to evil and back again, vacillating—especially if one believes in both ends of that line."

"Then a man like Reverend Gordon, according to what you say, because he believes in both God and Satan, could very well accept their existences as two separate facts," Ilene said, "without realizing they were each part of the same."

"You have a sharp mind, my dear," Joseph commented. "It is no wonder you have mastered your lessons so well. I have spoken of these theories to Shelia, and it was more difficult for your sister to grasp them."

"Shelia has not had the advantage of having been employed by Mrs. Phenwick," Ilene stated, "and being taught by her. I feel that I have had a great opportunity by being taken into the Phenwick household. Mrs. Phenwick is a very wise woman."

"I will say that for her," Joseph returned. "She is quite a marvelous person. I've said it to her face, I'll say it now. I have great admiration for her. Very few persons have accomplished what she has accomplished in one lifetime unless they had a very firm foundation and open mind. She told me that as a girl she spent many, many hours in the chapel at *La Chenille* where she developed a fine spiritual awareness; but her approach to matters of the spirit is quite different from that of Gordon."

As they drove farther down the road toward Lexington, they came to a hilly area. Beside the road a stream of water was flowing. Beyond the stream was a forest. High on the hill above was the skeleton of an old house. Joseph urged the horse to turn up an old dirt lane that led to the vicinity of the monstrous old skeleton. A sense of apprehension came over Ilene. Was it because she had seen an image of that structure in the distance, or was it because she was going there with Dr. Ornby?

The mansion was charred ruins. Chimneys still stood and were entwined by wild vines, but most of the house had been gutted by flame. It appeared ghostlike as it stood in silence.

"Who lived here?" asked Ilene.

"Nobody knows," Joseph informed her. "I suppose there is a record somewhere. The fire that destroyed it happened long after residents had abandoned it. Do you find it disagreeable being here?"

"Not necessarily."

"Because of the meadow and the shaded area down by the stream, I thought it would be a pleasant place for a picnic."

"How do you know nobody was living in this house at the time of the fire?" Ilene asked.

"Because the fire was set by Nancy Phenwick, prior to the time she married Cousin Peter," Joseph said.

"Miss Nancy set this house on fire? Why?"

"Because she was being menaced by an evil force," Joseph related. "That person died in the flames, trapped on the third floor."

"My goodness, I never knew," Ilene exclaimed.

"The family rarely speaks of it. Certainly Stuart doesn't, because it was his mother who was caught in the flames," Joseph continued. "Had it not been for Cousin Peter holding him back, Stuart would have dashed into the fire in an attempt to save her—and would have lost his life as well."

Do you mean that Miss Nancy was being tormented by Stuart's mother? "questioned Ilene.

"Yes. She didn't want Nancy to become a Phenwick woman," Joseph explained, "because she herself had not been accepted as one. Stuart and Gordon's mother was fanatically obsessed by her zealous belief in religion. There's a direct parallel between Gordon and his mother, Lillian. It is possible to be obsessed by other things, too, such as a belief in fairies or any other thing based on superstition."

"In fairies?" Ilene asked. "Meaning me?"

"In a sense, although I don't mean to suggest that you are fanatically obsessed by such a notion," Joseph remarked. "Still your leprechaun is most uncommon and leads one to think you might be obsessed by a peculiar thought."

Getting out of the carriage, Joseph tied the horse. They walked down the path that led to the meadow and the forest area. Many young birch trees had invaded the once cleared land. There was sufficient room to spread out a blanket, a cloth and the things the cook had packed for the lunch.

"Moorduke is very real to me," Ilene said, as if the thought had been bothering her, after a long period of silence. "I do see him and he does talk to me."

"I have no doubt that Gordon sees some sort of godly manifestation as well as a satanic one," Joseph commented. "At least he imagines he does."

"Moorduke is not in me imagination," Ilene stated emphatically. "He's very real."

"I'm not attacking Moorduke or any of your beliefs, child," the doctor explained. "Basically your belief in fairies is a belief in good, whereas those who become zealously obsessed by things of evil are apt to become violent and have a vengeful streak in their personality. A dual nature—two sides of possibly vast extremes. But I will say that your awareness of Moorduke is based on folk superstition, just as many of the religious fanatics ground their convictions on superstition."

"Superstition? Is that what you're saying, that I'm superstitious?" Ilene asked.

"Aren't you?"

"Maybe I am. But I cannot help myself about such things. How can I change?"

"You will change in time, once you completely outgrow your loneliness and become loved."

"Loved?" questioned Ilene.

"Yes. By a young man."

"Could you love me, Dr. Joseph?" she asked.

"I do love you, Ilene, in a special kind of way," Joseph expressed. "But I am not in love with you. The truth is, I am very much in love with—well, let me put it this way, I have a deep admiration for your sister Sheila."

"I thought as much. Alas, I would not do anything to hurt Sheila. She has had a suffering life, being parent and sister both. I do love her deeply. It would be wrong for me to attempt to lure you away from her. Still, if it had been you last night—"

"If it had been me last night?" questioned Joseph.

Ilene gasped. She had not meant to mention that situation. Quickly she explained what had happened in the church with Gordon.

"Why didn't you tell me this earlier?"

"Because I was frightened," Ilene said. "I wanted to put it from my mind, but it's very much there. I can't seem to eliminate it." She simply told of the attack by Gordon and his claiming that he was suddenly possessed by Satan, that it was the force of evil working through him that had caused him to attempt what he did. Realizing that the incident involving Moorduke coming to her aid would be difficult for Dr. Joseph to swallow, she avoided mentioning it. She said instead that she had managed to escape on her own.

"But as I said," Ilene continued, "I must confess, if it had been you last night I would have submitted to your physical will."

"Why, Ilene?"

"Because I find I have a strong fondness for you."

"You are a very moral person, you know right from wrong," Joseph said.

"Would it be wrong for me to submit if it were an expression of love?"

"Not if you felt it was right. But think, Ilene, would it be according to your principles?" Joseph asked.

"Perhaps I have a dual nature, too," Ilene said. "I do have moral principles, but, under certain circumstances, I would forsake them."

Joseph took her hand and put his other hand to her cheek, caressing it gently. "Dear Ilene, I have a deep respect and admiration for you. I, too, have moral principles, and very definitely believe in the strong force of love. The love I have for Sheila is the only expression of physical love I wish to experience. I know she is tied down in raising your younger brothers and sisters. I will wait. And my love will grow. Nor will I attempt to force myself physically upon her until a union has been sanctioned according to law. I hope one day you will be my sister-in-law. As such I will love you more than all the others. I confess my love for Sheila is so great that I could not foolishly express myself physically with anyone else and have a clear conscience."

"You make me feel ashamed of myself," Ilene sobbed. "You are so beautiful inside and out that I feel as if I have cheapened myself by even mentioning my desire for you."

"No, not cheapened, Ilene. Let us gather the things and go back to Boston," Joseph said. "I hope I have given you something to think about. One day when you have the courage to release Moorduke and end your belief in such superstitions, then you will open yourself to love and attracting the right man. Come along. I do have a few patients I must look in on this afternoon. I've enjoyed being with you, Ilene. I hope, in some way, I've been of help. As to Gordon, well, I'll have to think about my approach to his problem. If he is as you say he is, I feel he is in desperate need of help. Shall we go?"

Ilene bent forward and kissed the man on the cheek. "Thank you, Dr. Joseph. This is a day I will long remember."

CHAPTER THIRTEEN

The following day, Gordon Phenwick called again at Edward House. He encountered the stoic butler, Dietrich, who looked down on him with an attitude of defiance.

"I assure you I wish to see my aunt," Gordon explained. "And I promise I will be on my best behavior. You may take that information to her. Tell her that I am pleading for an audience."

Dietrich left the preacher in the foyer while he went to deliver the message.

"I believe under the circumstances, Dietrich," Patricia remarked after hearing the announcement, "that I would like you to remain. Will that be satisfactory to you?"

"Yes, madam, I shall inform Reverend Phenwick he may come up," the butler stated, and left the room.

Ilene retreated from the room at the same time as Dietrich, waiting in the shadowed hallway beyond, hidden from Gordon's view as he climbed the staircase.

Gordon stepped into Patricia's chamber with his usual arrogant attitude. She could tell he was attempting to put it under control.

Gordon mopped his broad brow and glanced back at Dietrich, who was standing by the window. "Is it not possible for us to be alone, Aunt Patricia?"

"I prefer that Dietrich remains, Joseph has given strict orders that I am not to be left alone," the old lady explained.

"But I will be here," Gordon said.

"I am quite aware of that, Nephew. Because of past performances," Patricia commented, "I feel it advisable for Dietrich to remain."

"Very well." Gordon pulled the chair close to his aunt's bed and spoke in a covered whisper. "I have come to confess something to you, Aunt Patricia?"

"A confession from you?" Patricia questioned. "That seems a bit of a change."

"Aunt Patricia, I'm in love. And I know that I have to have your approval as matriarch of this family."

"My approval? I didn't know you were interested in my approval about anything, Gordon."

"I am in this case, Aunt Patricia. You see, I am very much in love—and—well—let me say, I am excited to uncontrollable passion when I am near Ilene Dumphy."

"Uncontrollable passion? Do you equate passion with love?" asked Patricia.

"Isn't it part of it?" Gordon questioned. "Physical desire and fulfillment."

"Are you motivated strictly by physical desire and fulfillment, Gordon? Or do you have an inner longing, a true love for the girl?"

"I believe it is a true love—as true as love can be for me," he said.

"Gordon, are you unaware that your fanatical ways are repulsive to people? Especially to Ilene?"

"If I could learn to curb my zeal and change my ways, might I not encourage Ilene's interest?" Gordon sounded like a small boy pleading for a favor. His attitude altered. He squeezed his hands together until his fingers went white.

"At this point I can neither encourage nor discourage you, Gordon. One day of repentance is hardly sufficient to convince that the offender has changed his ways."

"Did Ilene tell you—?" Gordon caught himself.

"Did she tell me *what*?"

"She didn't mention the other night to you?"

"What about the other night, Gordon?"

"It is unimportant," Gordon stated. "The fact is, I want you to help me, Aunt Patricia. I have wrestled with my soul, like Jacob with the angel. I know that, of all the women I have ever met, only Ilene could make me happy."

"But could she make you change your ways?"

"My ways?"

"I would presume that you must know how offensive your proselytizing ways are to your family. Your zeal is often far too overwhelming to make you socially acceptable. Even your own brother is embarrassed by your behavior," Patricia stated. "I would think you would do far better to find a young woman who is convinced of your persuasions, your religious convictions."

"I am also a Phenwick, Aunt Patricia. I realize that part of my heritage is to be accepted by the family. Were I to marry Ilene, with your approval, I would be accepted for who I am."

"Perhaps for *who* you are but not necessarily *as* you are," Patricia said. "After your last visit to Edward House I would be reluctant ever to invite you to a social gathering— even if it were only a family reunion. You must consider that, Gordon. Now you're as docile as a kitten. What will you be ten minutes from now, by this afternoon or this evening? I have too much respect and interest in Ilene as an individual to encourage her in any direction I feel would be harmful for her. However, Gordon, as you say, you are a Phenwick. I cannot discount that fact. If you can prove to me that you can become socially acceptable, that you can curb your zeal, then I will consider being a liaison between you and Ilene."

The door opened and Marcia came barging in. "Oh, I'm sorry I didn't realize you had company, Grandmama."

"Come in, Marcia."

Gordon rose. "Good morning, Marcia. It's pleasant to see you today."

"Where is Ilene?" Marcia asked. "I thought she was sitting with you." She turned and saw Dietrich standing by the window.

"Ilene is having a recess," Patricia stated. "Gordon and I have just been having a private talk, which I believe has been concluded."

"It must have been Ilene I heard down in the library," Marcia commented. "I thought it was Dietrich. I can see he is here."

"Shall I get Miss Dumphy?" Dietrich asked as he went to the door.

"If you will, that will be kind," Patricia stated.

"I'll get her for you, Aunt Patricia," Gordon said. "I can see myself to the door, and the library is on the way. I'll ask her to come up."

Marcia exchanged a cautious look with Patricia. The girl wore an expression of alarm, knowing only too well of Gordon's habits. Patricia made a subtle nod of her head.

Once Gordon said goodbye and left the room, Patricia gave Dietrich instructions to remain in the vicinity of the library until Gordon was out of the house. The old lady asked Marcia to help her change position.

"Do you think it wise for Gordon to be with Ilene?" Marcia said, assisting her grandmother.

"You do not, I take it."

"I don't know how to react, Grandmama. Aren't you concerned about Ilene's welfare?"

"I am concerned for Ilene," Patricia remarked. "I am also concerned over Gordon. I believe my nephew needs help. He vacillates from one mood to another from day to day so drastically that I never know what to expect when he appears. Still I have a very fond aspiration that Ilene will become a Phenwick woman."

"You've decided on that, haven't you, Grandmama?"

"It would seem that Augusta has decided it. More and more the girl speaks of violets," Patricia said. "Violets are not in season now."

"According to what you told me," Marcia stated, "a Phenwick man must be accepted in the family as well as his wife. I refer to Stuart's parents. According to you, his mother was never accepted as a Phenwick woman."

"Gus, his father, was not much of a Phenwick man, either. He rebelled against his heritage. Oh, he became head of Medallion Enterprises, with his own father nearby, and he was a fairly good businessman. Nonetheless, he was not an ideal Phenwick man. He married Lillian out of spite for family tradition."

"Is that why Lillian was never accepted?"

"No, there were other things about Lillian," Patricia observed. "She did not make any attempt to alter her attitudes or her situation."

"Do you believe Gordon will ever alter his ways to the extent that you will accept him? Or his wife?" Marcia questioned.

"That I will have to take under deep consideration, my dear." Patricia sighed. "At the moment I am a bit groggy and feel the need of a nap. Will you sit with me until Ilene arrives?"

Marcia took a seat opposite the old woman.

One day the decisions concerning the acceptability of Phenwick women and men will rest on your shoulders, Marcia—yours and Nancy's," Patricia whispered. "That time may come sooner than you anticipate. But we will discuss that at another time."

Ilene was in the library when Gordon appeared at the door. At first she was alarmed by his presence. He presented a gentle smile and a congenial attitude. His manners were polite as he entered with an almost contrite expression.

"You will pardon me, Ilene," Gordon stated in a refined voice. "I have come to apologize for my behavior two nights ago. I have a troubled nature at times, when I am unable to resist the Devil and he is able to take hold of me. I fight—I desperately fight. I pray about it. At times a voice comes to me—whether it is the Holy Spirit or a guardian angel, I don't know—and it tells me that I allow the devil in by my uncontrollable passions. Yes, I'm a very emotional person, passionate, desirous of physical expression. I've never been able to resist the dominating power that takes hold of me. Today I am neither fish nor fowl, but the Gordon Phenwick who is in between. I feel I have had a calling from God, and that it is my duty to express it."

"You do express your calling from God, but I wonder if you don't also express a calling from Satan," Ilene said, "or at least what your concept of Satan is." She remembered the conversation she had had with Joseph, but felt herself ill-equipped to repeat his philosophy.

"If you could only understand me, Ilene, you would know the troubled soul that lies within this flesh," Gordon announced. "I do help people. I reach into the gutter and scoop them up and give them something to hope for, to live for. But I'm also a mortal with weaknesses and involve myself with nefarious lusting. If I had married younger and had had a regular outlet for my passions, I might not be as desperate as I am today."

"You are desperate, Reverend Phenwick, I know that by what you did the other night," Ilene related. "You were no human being, you were an animal possessed by the force of evil."

"I know. I know only too well." He dropped to his knees. "Please forgive me. I beg you to forgive me. Don't you understand how urgently I need you to say that what I did did not offend you."

"But it did offend me, Reverend Phenwick."

"Then I am truly sorry, truly sorry indeed. Please, Ilene, please help me!" Gordon pleaded. "I have a deep passion for you. I'm reaching out like a drowning man. Will you let me sink?"

"What is it you want of me?"

"At the moment, your forgiveness; ultimately—well—it's too early to go into that. I have confessed myself to you. What more can I do?"

The door opened and Stuart entered.

Quickly Gordon scrambled to get to his feet.

He was embarrassed. His face grew red with humiliation.

"I'm sorry if I interrupted," Stuart commented.

"My dear brother," Gordon returned, trying to be as friendly as possible, but he was wild-eyed and possessed with passion.

"Dietrich mentioned you were in here," Stuart stated. "It seems Marcia is ready for Ilene to return to sit with Aunt Patricia."

"I'm ready," Ilene replied.

Gordon had begun to tremble. A fierce anger was welling within him. Was he vindictive toward his brother, or was his antagonism toward Ilene, who seemed anxious to escape from his presence? Whatever it was that triggered him, he could feel the rumble of anxiety and emotion within himself.

"Yes, she must go back to the old lady upstairs and sit as if she were in a grave watching her die," Gordon snapped.

"Ilene was hired to attend Aunt Patricia, Gordon," Stuart commented. "That is her position in this house."

"Yes, but her youth and beauty being captive in that one dismal room is regretful."

"Would you prefer she was on her hands and knees scrubbing like a common charwoman?" Stuart returned.

"I have overstayed my visit," Gordon declared, barely able to control the fury that was building within him. "I'm anxious to get about other business. Excuse me."

CHAPTER FOURTEEN

"What was that all about?" Stuart asked as he heard the outside door close behind his brother.

"I'm not certain, Mr. Phenwick," Ilene replied.

"From all appearances, it looked as if Gordon were proposing to you when I entered this room," Stuart commented.

"Proposing to me?" Ilene questioned. "No such thing. Besides, I would certainly reject such a proposal."

"Why, my child?"

"Because I find your brother disagreeable."

"Speaking in my brother's defense, I know he is unorthodox in many things he does, his ways are peculiar; but because he is my brother, I feel a deep kinship to him, a closeness I cannot overlook."

"He is a most unusual man," Ilene stated. "If it were not for his queer beliefs—well—I find such things repulsive."

"No doubt, Ilene. Still I think you should consider what it would mean for you to marry Gordon," Stuart said.

"To marry him?" Ilene asked incredulously.

"What it would mean for you to become a Phenwick woman," Stuart continued. "It would surely lift you from your status as a serving girl into an elegant lady. I've spoken with Aunt Patricia, and I know it is her desire that you become a Phenwick woman."

"To marry Reverend Phenwick? Oh no, sar, I could nay do that," Ilene returned, an expression of disgust on her face. "Couldn't I possibly become a Phenwick woman if I were to marry someone like Dr. Joseph Ornby who is really a member of the family?"

"Joe? I don't believe it would be the same." Stuart chuckled. "He is a lovable person, I have no doubt, and probably more inclined to your way of thinking in many respects. While in the lineage of Jane Phenwick, he is not considered a Phenwick man. If you like, I will speak to Aunt Patricia about it."

For several moments Ilene meditated on the subject as pictures of that dreadful evening in the church flashed into her mind. Mustering confidence, she related to Stuart exactly what had happened that night, sparing no details.

Stuart was shocked. "I don't believe it. This of Gordon? You're not making this up, Ilene?"

"It truly happened, sar," she replied. "I don't know how I made it back to Edward House with all the terror and torment that was going on within me." She sighed.

"That puts a different light on the matter, doesn't it?" Stuart observed. "It would be difficult after an ordeal like that for a man to endear himself to a young lady."

"Extremely difficult, Mr. Phenwick, sar," Ilene replied. "It's not that he's unhandsome, for in my eyes he is. It's only on the outside. It's what's on the inside that frightens me. He's like two different people. The other night, I was aware of a person who was filled with religion, a man of God. In just a few moments he changed into an animal-like monster as though he were an instrument of Satan. That was the most frightening part about it, seeing a man change like that before my very eyes—change into a demon."

"My God!" exclaimed Stuart. "If he did that to you, someone known to his family, imagine what he has attempted or actually accomplished with others. This is very distressing news. Still I find that I question the veracity of your story when you speak of the intervention of a leprechaun."

"I can see where that would make a difference. I'm not lying," Ilene stated. "I can't explain Moorduke. Maybe there's two sides of me, too. Two sides as queer as the sides of Reverend Phenwick."

"Have you spoken to anyone else about this?"

"Not in detail as I have told you," Ilene explained. "Except for Dr. Joseph."

"I prefer that you didn't relate it to anyone else until I have had time to think the matter over," Stuart stated. "Now I realize how desperately ill my brother is. If he has these two sides to his character, the God and Satan parts, then there is no telling where he is headed. I have compassion for him, but I know that he needs to be helped. I don't believe, Ilene, that you are the one to do it. I am his closest relative. It is up to me to find assistance for him. Now I believe you had better get upstairs. Marcia needs to be excused."

"Thank you for your understanding, Mr. Phenwick," Ilene said. "As for Moorduke, I know it was a mistake me mentionin' him from the very beginning. I didn't mean to. It just slipped out."

"I understand, Ilene. We all have our little peculiarities and things that are distinctly us," Stuart commented. "I don't think you should consider yourself in the same position as Gordon. Your Moorduke is apparently quite harmless. We'll discuss the matter later. Hurry along now."

Stuart sat in a chair as he watched Ilene leave the room. He sighed deeply and ran his fingers through his hair as the anguishing thought of dealing with his brother's problem haunted him.

CHAPTER FIFTEEN

Throughout that day Stuart wrestled with his thoughts, his deep concern about Gordon and how he must handle the situation. He did not want to concern Patricia with the problem, or any of his other relatives, until he was certain of the gravity of the situation.

That evening he went out in hopes of finding his brother. Realizing that Gordon spent the early summer evenings in the Common, that was the first place he looked. He wanted to watch and observe, to see if he could detect any subtle differences in Gordon's character and outlook.

When Stuart arrived at the park, a group was gathered around Gordon. The horns and tambourines bellowed forth while lusty voices sang a hymn of joy and praise. Happiness came from the music and the people seemed to be enjoying themselves. The second selection dealt with a very morbid aspect of the bloody death of Jesus. As Stuart observed, he saw the expressions of the onlookers and how their emotions changed with the new hymn. He also noticed how Gordon altered in his manner. This was not the first time he had watched his brother during such occasions, and he felt that part of it was a performance Gordon was putting on—studied gestures and articulation, a mood that would emotionally impress his audience and stir them to the level of passion he was experiencing.

Viewing the scene as objectively as possible, Stuart realized that a definite transformation had taken place, not only in his brother's appearance but in his overall character. The wild actions that he used, the gyrations, the thumping of his chest with his fist, the hollering, the rage that increased in his voice moving him to the verge of being hysterical, all these became obvious to Stuart as he reached the conclusion that his brother was either an extremely good actor or there very definitely were two sides to his character.

When Gordon's eyes met those of his brother, the preacher did not seem to recognize Stuart. He aimed an accusing finger at Stuart, claiming that he was a sinner who must repent and find his way into grace.

Stuart pushed his way through the crowd until he stood before Gordon. Gordon's hand reached out and practically touched his brother's face.

"Are you speaking to me?" Stuart asked.

"Oh yes, poor sinner! Get to your knees and repent of your foolish ways!" Gordon exclaimed.

"Gordon! Do you know who I am?"

"I know you're a sinner," Gordon cried, his eyes glassy as if he were seeing beyond the physical appearance of Stuart and into the depths of his soul.

"Who am I, Gordon?"

"You are an unrighteous pagan! A lustful sinner!"

"What is my name?"

"Your name is legion, for you are the devil incarnate!"

"What is my name, Gordon?" Stuart reached forward and grabbed his brother by the vest.

The preacher quickly raised his hand and slapped his brother to force him to unhand his garment. "You have been smitten by the Lord Jesus Christ, in and through me! Now to your knees and repent, for the Holy Spirit has moved upon you and you must be saved!"

Stuart backed his way through the crowd while the others gathered around. He watched. Gordon did not even seem to notice that he had moved away. His attention went to another nearby as if that were the person he had slapped.

By the time Stuart reached the periphery of the crowd, the sting still tingling his cheek, he was back so far that he could just see Gordon's hands as they flew into the air. Yet he could hear the almost maniacal chatter of Gordon's preaching. He must immediately go to find Joseph Ornby. To delay might be disastrous for everyone in the Phenwick family, particularly for Gordon.

Stuart had never encountered any insane persons. It had been his good fortune not to have done so. However, Gordon's behavior was so similar to that of his mother as Stuart recalled from his boyhood, that a very disquieting sensation came with a realization that Gordon was not in his right mind.

The Ornby home was large and spacious. It was not the opulent structure that Edward House was, nor did it have the pretentions. Yet it was comfortable for Dr. Ted, Louise and the children. Augustus, the second son, was away in Europe; Collin, the next, lived in Cambridge; the two daughters Mary and Ruth were married and both lived outside of Boston with their husbands. Joseph still remained with his parents, having a suite of three rooms on the second floor.

When Stuart arrived, he was shown to Joseph's room. They shook hands and exchanged a few lighthearted comments. Stuart had wanted Joseph to join his club, but the young doctor had declined, saying that he would not have time for such activities or exercise. Again Stuart broached the subject, again Joseph declined.

"I don't believe membership in your club was the purpose of your coming here this evening, Stuart," the doctor commented. "Am I mistaken?"

"You're not mistaken," Stuart replied. "I have come with several grave matters on my mind, the most significant of which involves my brother."

"What about Gordon?"

"I'm deeply concerned about him." Stuart explained what had occurred in the church between Gordon and Ilene, then went on to relate his own experience in the Common a short while before.

"Ilene informed me of the incident that occurred in the church," Joseph said after listening to his cousin's narration. "Now with what you tell me about Gordon, I can believe that such a thing actually happened. It is only the girl's insistence about that blamed leprechaun that annoys me."

"Forget about the leprechaun," Stuart returned. "That is just a figment of her imagination—a fantasy. The important thing we must deal with now is Gordon. I admit what I saw tonight frightened me."

"Not without good cause," Joseph stated.

"I doubt there is much we can do for him at this point, my cousin. The best that can be done is to keep him under observation. So little is known about the processes of the mind—particularly the malfunctioning aspects of it. There are studies and experiments being done in Europe. But little is known about insanity—or at least the treatment of it. History is filled with barbaric, inhuman accounts of how such poor souls were treated. The notorious Bedlam is a classical example. But we simply don't know what causes this quirk in the human mind."

"A quirk?"

"What else is it, Stuart?" asked Joseph. "I have read and reread *The Mysteries of Rosea Hackleby*. Far from being a scientific text, but the old lady put forth a strong argument about possession particularly in relationship to our distant kin, Rachel Phenwick, As you describe Gordon, he shows similar signs in behavior—except, according to Rosea, not only another personality but another voice came from Rachel when she was under possession by the alien spirits. This would not seem to be the case with Gordon. He definitely appears to have two sides to his own personality."

"He didn't even know me this evening," Stuart said. "I was horrified at his reaction. As far back as I can remember into childhood, Gordon has always had this religious streak—like that of my mother. I always simply believed that that was Gordon, and there was nothing one could do about it."

"It is Gordon," Joseph returned. "I suspect something within him is in rebellion with that righteous nature. The situation with Ilene would lead me to suspect his carnal nature is as uncontrolled and unpredictable as his moral nature. He is in conflict within himself. Could it possibly be that the one person he is most desperately trying to save *is* himself? I will make a point of going to see him for an interview—and if he will permit, an examination."

"An examination?"

"A physical examination. I don't know what it will prove, but there might possibly be some correlation between a physical problem or defect and his mental state."

"What sort of physical problem?"

"My dear Stuart, I have no idea. It is just a thought," Joseph smiled reassuringly. "I want you to know that I will do all I can to help your brother—before—"

"Before?"

"Well, for the present let us be as optimistic as we can, shall we?"

Stuart swallowed hard. He thanked his cousin, shook his hand and explained that he could find his way out.

CHAPTER SIXTEEN

Reverend Gordon Phenwick had acquired several pieces of property, including three choice lots on Back Bay. He owned at least four houses of considerable size throughout the Boston area as well as property in the area inhabited by the extremely poor. A clever businessman, his ways were not always the most conventional and he ruthlessly administered his affairs, showing little compassion when a tenant would fall behind with his rent.

Small, wiry Angus Parson was his attorney and business administrator, an unsavory man at best. It was Parson who handled the dirty work of collecting the rent and forcing necessary evictions. The short, bald man with a full moustache possessed beady eyes that rodentlike seemed to be aware of all directions at once. Miserly, he even bilked Gordon of funds, since the preacher was not one for mathematical detail and accepted the books presented to him by Parson.

Each morning Parson would arrive at the church and make a report to Gordon. Progressively he could observe the change coming over the relatively young preacher. Gordon tried to be a cold pragmatist, but his emotional nature was such that his moods changed so regularly

Parson realized something was drastically wrong. Instinctively Gordon must have been aware of his own erratic nature. Since his mind was usually less muddled in the early morning, that was the time he selected to go over affairs with Parson. But Gordon was not so foolish that he depended entirely upon Parson and many of his legal matters were handled by his cousin, Daniel Ornby, the attorney. He considered it a check-and-balance system.

Joseph Ornby knew Gordon had a business conference each morning between eight and nine-thirty at the church. The best time to catch him in was immediately after Parson left. The doctor remained on the opposite side of the street until he saw the small man leave, a stern expression on his face as he suspiciously glanced about the area before departing the old wooden building.

"Good morning, Gordon," Joseph called as he entered the side door to the church and went immediately to the office. "May I disturb you for a while?"

"Ah, Joseph," Gordon said enthusiastically. It was a rarity that any member of his family entered his church. "This is a pleasant surprise." He shook the man's hand. "Welcome to the house of God."

"Thank you, Gordon," Joseph returned. "Do you have time for a little chat?"

"My day starts early with services at the mission," Gordon remarked, offering his cousin a seat opposite the old wooden desk. "This time of the day is the best to catch me at ease. What can I do for you?"

"Since we are bachelor members of the family," Joseph said cautiously, "I thought we should take

161

more time to know each other. I've been meaning to call on you for some time."

"It surprises me you're not married yet, Joseph," Gordon commented. "I trust you're not living in sin."

"Far from it. With my father away in Europe for the summer, I have had a very busy schedule handling his patients as well as my own." Joseph laughed. "That hardly leaves much time for sinning. And you?"

"Me? I'm a minister of God, a disciple of Jesus Christ," Gordon answered. "I live above sin and transgression."

"Do you?"

Gordon stared coldly at him. Suddenly he broke into a jolly roar of laughter. "You obviously don't understand what it means to be a man in my position."

"Are you a celibate like the Catholic priests?"

Gordon's eyes widened and his eyebrows lowered in that studied expression he used so well. "Protestant ministers are not required to be celibates. Why do you ask such a question?"

"I was curious. You have always struck me as being an emotional person," Joseph stated, leaning back in the chair. "Usually such a person has a strong need for physical outlet."

"Are you insinuating something?" Gordon snapped.

"Not in the least." Joseph glanced over at the rumpled covers on the cot. "Do you sleep here at night?"

Gordon looked at the cot. "Not at night. Occasionally I have a nap in the afternoon."

"That cot appears to have had a considerable amount of use," Joseph observed.

"It was old when I moved it in. Why are you asking these things, Joseph? You're up to something, I can tell."

"I suppose you've considered marriage, Gordon."

"The thought has entered my mind. Why do you ask?"

"Can't find the right girl?"

"I have found one who greatly interests me," Gordon confessed, "but she rebuffs me."

"Do you have doubts about yourself?"

"What kind of question is that?"

"I mean, as a man who can function as a husband."

"I'm not inexperienced." Gordon's eyes were becoming fiery. A sudden change. "Satan has a way of tempting Christians into carnal lusting. That's the way he gets control over them."

"Are you suggesting the reproductive urge is the work of Satan?"

"Not necessarily when such acts are for the purpose of reproduction," Gordon stated, "but when they are the expression of wanton lusting, yes. Oh, I know how Satan tempts and lures the innocent. I've seen the desperate results of his prompting."

"You speak as if you are quite familiar with him."

"Satan tempted Jesus Christ in the desert," Gordon explained. "He tempts all of His followers."

"Meaning that you've been tempted?"

"I am a mortal!" Gordon declared, his anger rising. "I know the outrageous ways of the flesh! Why, Satan's ministers violate the sanctity of the human body in a disgusting act of debasing the soul. It's part of the ritual of Satanism."

"Satanism?"

"The worship of Satan!" Gordon glared and pounded his fist on the desk top. "The warlock, Satan's advocate, takes carnal pleasure with whomever he pleases to glorify the master of darkness. He is the pawn of the great tormentor, defiling the persons of both women and men. Satan makes him do it! Oh, that is why I am on such a crusade against Satan!"

Joseph stared at the preacher with an almost accusing look. "Are you on such a crusade *against* Satan, Gordon?"

"I deplore him."

"Do you take physical gratification from both female and male?"

Gordon reddened. Tormented confusion twisted his face. Twice he started to speak, but caught himself. "How dare you come to me with such a question?"

"I was simply wondering how you managed to be such an authority on such things," Joseph explained. "I was curious to know if Satan had tempted you in such perverse directions."

"Fiend! Why have you come here?"

"To visit, Gordon. You may ask me about my private life, if you wish. I have nothing to hide."

"Hypocrite!"

"No. Innocent. I have heard such things exist, but I have never experimented. Have you?"

Gordon sputtered. His features became so distorted that he appeared to be wearing a Satanic mask. With teeth tightly gripped together and lips pulled back to expose them, he practically hissed. His fist banged the desk top again and his eyes seemed as if they were about to bulge out of his head. His rage became intense before he was able to regain control. Slowly his features returned to normal as if the question had finally sunk in and had shaken him out of his desperate reaction.

"I am a minister of God," Gordon recited, his voice still shaking, but attempting a calmness that had not been there. "I am offended that you would even suggest such a thing. When I spoke of the devil, I was speaking in abstractions. I know what the prescribed ritual for Satanism is. That is why I am so devoted to my mission of salvation."

Again Joseph studied his cousin's reactions with interest, "Ilene Dumphy and I—"

"That harlot!" Gordon yelled. "Don't mention her name in this sacred place."

"On what do you base your accusation?"

"Has she spoken to you about me?" His eyes became shifty again and his lips trembled.

"If you think she is a harlot, why would you ask her to marry you?"

"Did she tell you that?"

"That was the impression you gave her," Joseph said softly. "Don't you find her physically attractive? Aren't you aroused by her presence?"

"She must be saved! She is one of the great unclean! Oh, it grieves me to see such a wayward soul in torment!"

"Gordon," Joseph said sharply, "Ilene Dumphy is neither a harlot nor unclean. She is a fine girl, possessed of charm, beauty and wit. But you will never succeed with her by brutishly attempting to force yourself on her."

"She told you!" Gordon raged. "She lied! It never happened!"

"*What* never happened?"

Gordon stared at him, realizing he had said the wrong thing. "Whatever she told you happened."

"I want to help you, Gordon." Joseph spoke softly in a well-modulated voice.

"I don't need any of your damned help!"

"Don't you?" Joseph rose and went to put his hand on Gordon's shoulder. "I do want to help you, Gordon. I can see the kind of state you are in. I wish to lead you to the salvation of your emotional self. You are obviously troubled."

Gordon knocked his cousin's hand away. "I don't want your help," he sneered. "I know why you're here. It's because of what she told you. Well, you can go elsewhere."

"If you'd only cooperate."

"If you'd only go straight to hell!" Gordon roared. Violence shook his body. His eyes bulged again and his brow changed to give him a furious expression. "Get out of here! How dare you desecrate the house of God! How dare you make slanderous accusations, taking the word of a common street girl against your own flesh and blood? I demand that you never enter this house of God again, not until you are ready to apologize—to repent of your outrageous sins."

Joseph looked deeply into the distraught man's eyes. "Is Jesus Christ truly your savior, Gordon? Or are you playing a hypocritical game with yourself?"

"Out! Get out, you heathen!" Gordon shoved him from the office. "I will not even taint my soul to pray for you. I believe you quite mad! Mad! Mad! Mad! Do you hear?"

"Yes, I hear, Gordon," Joseph said at the door. "I hear who is speaking. There's an image about the pot calling the kettle an evil color. Well, this kettle is highly polished compared to the pot, I fear. Good day, Gordon."

Gordon grabbed a letter opener and flung it at the door. It rattled with a dull clatter as it hit the floor. He remained bracing himself against the desk as he listened for Joseph's retreating footsteps and the closing of the outside door.

"Lucifer! Lucifer! How have you gotten such a strong hold over me?" Gordon shrieked. "My mind, my mind—what's becoming of it? I believe in Jesus Christ. I do believe! Why then have you become so much stronger and taken dominance over me! Oh God, my body aches for release!"

Joseph made his way toward the street when his attention was attracted to two children playing in the yard beside the church. The boy was no more than twelve, the girl younger. Then he glanced to the window of Gordon's office. His cousin was standing by it, watching the children.

A lustful expression had come to Gordon's face as he obscenely rubbed his hand down over his body.

Fortunately the children's mother appeared and called the children away, reprimanding them for playing on church property.

Joseph was confused and felt helpless. With his father away, the only person with whom he believed he could speak was his Uncle Daniel. But he did not.

CHAPTER SEVENTEEN

Patricia continued to instruct Ilene in the ways of being a lady. For the most part, the girl made fine progress. Her brogue was completely gone and her carriage and manners were elegant. Periodically Ilene would fall back into her old ways, and occasionally use words that were a reflection of her background. But Patricia was a strict teacher. The old lady was proud of the progress she had made. Yet the nearer to perfection Ilene became in her lessons, the more Patricia realized that her project was about to come to an end. What would she do then?

"Tell me, Ilene," the old woman stated one morning, "do you still enjoy visits with Moorduke? You haven't mentioned him in some time."

"Oh, I still have visits with him, Mrs. Phenwick," the girl replied, "but as to enjoying them, that is a different matter."

"How so?"

"He is constantly harping on me, berating me about this and that," Ilene explained. "He doesn't encourage me to become a lady. And sometimes I wonder if he isn't right."

"Put such notions from your head, child," Patricia exclaimed. "You have learned your lessons well and in a remarkably short period of time."

"Moorduke appears less and less often," Ilene related. "I believe he has found other interests. However, I do know he is homesick. I believe that is why he stays away. But he still brings me violets. Even when he doesn't appear himself, I receive the fragrance of violets and know that he is somewhere nearby."

"Perhaps it isn't Moorduke who is bringing you violets, Ilene."

"Oh, but it must be. It's his way." Ilene went to the window and looked out into the garden. "But they aren't real violets, are they? I realize that now. They're only imaginary—as I suspect Moorduke is. I've mentioned this to Moorduke and he becomes offended, telling me that he will abandon me if I don't change me—my—way of thinking. He says it's one thing to be a lady on the outside, it's another to forget my heritage on the inside. He doesn't understand. Sometimes I don't understand." She suddenly turned around. "Why did you say it might not be Moorduke who is bringing me the scent of violets?"

The old lady attempted to laugh. It made her cough. "My dear Ilene, has it occurred to you that there may be other mysterious forces working around you? Dear Augusta—"

"Augusta? Do you mean Augusta Phenwick?"

"It is a belief that Augusta's spirit hovers about potential Phenwick women and makes itself known with the scent of violets."

"Isn't that as fanciful as my belief in Moorduke?"

"Perhaps. But isn't Moorduke real to you?"

"Yes."

"It may be senility approaching at a rapid pace, but I have faith in Augusta," Patricia stated.

"But why me?"

"That I don't know, child." Patricia looked away. "I wonder what's become of Gordon. He hasn't been to call in some time."

"He is a very strange man, Mrs. Phenwick—you'll pardon me for saying so."

"But he is a Phenwick."

Dietrich interrupted their conversation to announce that Dr. Joseph Ornby had arrived to examine the old lady.

"Why don't you take a recess while Joseph is here, Ilene? There is no need for you to sit with me while he makes his examination."

"I would like a bit of a stroll in the garden. It is a beautiful day," Ilene said.

Joseph exchanged warm glances with Ilene as he entered and she left the room. He watched her dance down the stairway before he turned back into the room.

"You are fascinated by her, aren't you, Joseph?"

"What?"

"That's what I thought," Patricia remarked. "I wonder if Augusta would stretch a point and consider you a Phenwick man."

"I beg your pardon, Aunt Patricia."

"Nothing. Just the ramblings of an old lady approaching senility," Patricia remarked. "I've lived far too long. I'm tired. Still I would like to see Ilene happy before—well, before whatever happens. Have you given thoughts to love, Joseph?"

Joseph blushed. "I believe I am in love now."

"Ah, not with—?"

"With Ilene's sister Sheila."

"Oh." Patricia sounded disappointed.

"But there are complications."

"Love unfortunately has many complications,"

170

Patricia remarked. "That is what makes it last. Were it not for the minor obstacles, I fear love would become monotonous before it really had time to age. Like good wine, love takes time to mature. Still I have known the first signs of it to grow quite rapidly."

"An interesting bit of philosophy, Aunt Patricia," Joseph said, "but I didn't come here for that sort of discourse today. I have a busy schedule."

"You always have a busy schedule. Take time to live, Joseph."

"I'll remember that, Aunt Patricia," he stated as he began to examine her.

"My grandson Gregory, while he is doing well with the Medallion business in London, I fear spends much time in frivolous living. How could he help it with his mother and Joanna encouraging him? Still I trust one day he will meet the right girl and—" She stopped.

"It's better if you don't speak, Aunt Patricia. I cannot get an accurate count if you're talking."

After the examination, Joseph pulled a chair up to the bed. He took the old lady's hand.

"How are you fixed for bravery today, Aunt Patricia?"

"What is it, Joseph?"

"I want to be honest with you and not deceive," he said solemnly. "Your health is failing. You show no signs of improvement. I fear you will never get out of bed again."

"Not even to sit by my window?"

"Perhaps that, but only with assistance."

"I've always been one to take a realistic attitude toward life, Joseph," she said. "What you're trying to tell me is that I'm dying, isn't that the case?"

"Not exactly."

"But I am. I know that. I think from the moment we're born we begin the process of dying," Patricia stated. "Some of us are even self-destructive as if we were attempting to hurry the process. I wonder why that is. Well, I appreciate your candor, Joseph. But may I make a special request?"

"What is it?"

"That you let it be our secret—just yours and mine. I'll let the others know in my own way," she commented. "Oh, what I would give to attend just one more ball—a lavish affair with all my friends gathered around. Alas, all my friends are gone or have become as decayed as I have. Well—if I couldn't dance and be gay at my party, I think it would prove to be very dull. No. Parties are out for me." She thought a moment as a coy smile came to her lips. "But I do have one mission left. Why did I not think of it before?"

"What is it, Aunt Patricia?"

"I never divulge my schemes until they're worked out in my head," Patricia said. "And I've just gotten the idea. When you leave will you go across to Marcia's room and ask her to come in here? Let Ilene remain out in the fresh air a little longer."

Patricia eyed the brandy decanter after Joseph left the room. She did not have the strength to lift herself from the bed. She knew his prognosis was correct, but it did not distress her.

"You wanted me, Grandma*ma*?" Marcia asked, showing distinct signs of her pregnancy. "I was lying down."

"Sorry to disturb you, dear," the old lady commented, "but I want you to write some letters for me, if you don't mind."

"Whatever you wish, Grandma*ma*." Marcia got the writing paper and sat at the desk.

"I want you to write to both of my daughters, Susannah and Rebecca. Inform them that I do not believe I will live through another winter."

"But Grandma*ma*—"

"Do as you're told and don't become emotional," Patricia said. "If you could comprehend the horror I endure being confined to this bed, you would be happy for me. That is neither here nor there. I want you to explain to Susannah and Rebecca that I would very much like to see them again. Furthermore, I wish to see Kate and John Collier—tell Rebecca that. And I would very much like to visit again with your brother Gregory." She smiled. "And that ruggedly handsome man that Susannah married—"

"Jim Cornhill."

"Yes, that's the one. I would like to see him again," Patricia stated. "I got a very good feeling when he was here. He is the kind of man I always found interesting. I don't want to alarm them, but tell them I would like to see them all as soon as possible."

"Did Dr. Joseph—?"

"Now now, Marcia, what Joseph and I discussed was of a professional nature," Patricia commented. "I know I am steadily weakening. I cannot describe the pain I suffer or the longing I have to be out of this bed."

"You want to—I mean—"

"Marcia dearest, I have always wanted to do many things," the old lady stated, "and I've usually done them—sooner or later. Sometimes not soon enough—sometimes not late enough. But I've done them." She chuckled to herself. "Oh, and while you're at it, write a special note to your brother. Tell Gregory that I am most anxious to see him. He is my closest male heir and I have something special I wish to give to him. Make it sound urgent enough for him to put aside whatever else is occupying his time and come."

"Gregory?" Marcia looked up at the woman. "I very much would like to see Gregory again, too. He will be amused to see my swollen belly. Dear, dear Gregory—I pray that one day he will marry, too, and have children."

"You know, my dear, I have been thinking about that myself."

"What do you mean, Grandma*ma*?" Marcia knew Patricia well enough to know that she did not make such mysterious statements without a reason.

"Simply that I have a concern for my grandson's welfare and happiness. Frivolous games are delightful for a while, but there comes a time when we all must take things seriously," Patricia commented, "both life and death."

"Grandma*ma*?"

The door burst open and Ilene entered with a wonderful exuberance. Then remembering she was in the invalid's room, she pretended a more sober attitude.

"Tell Gregory," Patricia said after observing Ilene, "that I very much want him to sit for his portrait while he's here. It's a shame we have nothing but that horrible photograph of him."

Marcia looked from the old lady to Ilene and back again. A dim smile came to her lips. "Once he says he'll come, I'll contact Raymond Nelson. His work is gaining great acclaim."

"Dear Raymond. I wonder why he never comes

to call on me much anymore," Patricia said. "Perhaps it distresses him to see me withering as I am when he knew me in much better days."

Ilene went to the window and breathed deeply of the fresh air. Then she twirled about into the room.

"Did you bring the scent of violets in with you, Ilene?" asked Patricia.

Marcia looked at the girl.

"No, they were already here when I arrived," Ilene replied. "What a happy fragrance they are, too."

Marcia watched the girl as the excitement of laughter moved through her.

CHAPTER EIGHTEEN

Sun-bleached, golden blond hair blew in the wind. Eyes squinted out sunlight. White teeth glistened as he sang. The man was firmly constructed, broad-shouldered, tall with an imposing physique. The wind lashed his open blouse against the fine definition of masculine pulchritude beneath. Thick lips, even when not singing, were permanently curved into a smile. His inner happiness could not be disguised.

The ship, *The Patricia*, was nearing Boston harbor. Land was still a tiny speck in the distance. It had been some time since Gregory Phenwick had been in Boston. The anticipation of seeing his beloved sister Marcia excited him. Distant memories flashed into his mind's eye as he recalled scenes from his past, pictures going back before the time he and Marcia were adopted into the Phenwick family. Now he was without a doubt a staunch member, respected and admired by most of the others. He had become a good businessman as well as an admired man about London. His admirers were many. Unfortunately he often found himself being the prey of fortune seekers who wished to marry into the Phenwick name. He was leery, cautious not to encourage. Because he had such great self-confidence, he wanted to choose, not be the chosen. Still Gregory enjoyed life and loved the joy of being young and desirable.

Big Jim Cornhill strode up beside the boy. Jim's hair had turned silver, but his features were as ruggedly handsome as they had been in years past. He had rejected taking the Phenwick name when he married Susannah, displaying the pride he took in his own humble ancestry. His wife professionally went by the name of Phenwick, but privately she was more than pleased to be known as Mrs. Cornhill. Jim put a thick hand on Gregory's shoulder to interrupt the song the youth had been singing.

"Happily anticipatin' arrivin' in Boston, are ya?" Jim questioned. "'Twill be good to see Marcia again."

"Is Mother staying below?"

"The wind is too severe for the lass," Jim replied. "She will wait until we tie in at the pier. Besides, she believes the sun ages her skin, and she wants to appear young as ever."

Gregory laughed.

"D'ya miss the lasses ye left behind, lad?"

"The world is filled with pretty girls, Jim," Gregory returned. "You should know that."

"Aye, I do."

"Fact is, I've been doing some serious thinking on this voyage," Gregory continued. "Being a butterfly in the social scene is enjoyable for a while, but I think it time I was seriously considering settling into a more stable way of life."

"Are ye thinkin' o' marriage?"

"One day soon," the youth replied. "The first step is to find the right woman."

"Aye, one who will make a proper Phenwick woman, eh?"

"I never thought Mother was that concerned about tradition," Gregory stated, "but she has spoken to me several times about the subject of marriage. I know it is on her mind."

"She's a brave lass, at her age plannin' on doin' a concert in Boston," Jim commented. "She still has her old style, but her fingers—aye, they've be-cum a bit tired over the years."

"It's the best thing that could have happened to her," Gregory said with laughter. "Bless Stuart for arranging the concert. Besides, I fear when she sees Grandmother, she is liable to become depressed, realizing how old she has become. Marcia writes that the old lady is bedridden and has been so for quite a while. We'll all have to do our best to cheer her."

"Her? Meanin' your grandmother?"

"And Mother." Gregory's smile only slightly diminished. "It'll be good to see Stuart, Peter, and Nancy again—and their boys. I can't imagine how they've grown."

Jim knew the concern Gregory had for Susannah. He tried to make light of it. Still the evidence that Susannah was aging was ever present and could not be denied.

Stuart was at the dock when *The Patricia* moored. He was first aboard and greeted Gregory with the handshake that had been of special significance to them over the years. Then the men threw their arms about each other and embraced.

Susannah appeared from below, elegantly attired in yellow. Her hair had lost its previous golden luster and she moved with a slowness of step. Still she was lovely. The lines of time simply put more character in her face. She wore a white bonnet to protect her hair from the wind and was only too delighted to be going ashore. Holding Gregory's arm, she made her way down the gangplank to be greeted by Marcia, Nancy and her four sons. Peter had been feeling under the weather and was unable to meet the ship.

"You will all stay at Edward House," Marcia announced, clinging tightly to Susannah after she had kissed Gregory with a warm greeting.

The moment of shock for Susannah occurred when she entered Patricia's room. The aged and withered woman was hardly recognizable to her daughter. She went to the bed, sat on it and embraced Patricia. Gregory and Jim remained just inside the door with Stuart and Marcia.

"Be careful, missus," Ilene warned, "she is a bit fragile and is sometimes filled with pain."

"It's all right, Ilene," Patricia said. "To hold my daughter in my arms again can only be beautiful pain. My dearest Susannah, you haven't changed a bit."

"That's not true, Mother," Susannah returned, "but it's kind of you to say so." She kissed her mother, then rose from the bed.

"Grandmother!" Gregory exclaimed as he went to greet the old lady, kissing her on the cheek and gently stroking her.

"Can this be Gregory? Oh my dear. What a handsome man you've become, big and full-shouldered. An Adonis! Not only will I have Raymond paint your portrait, but I'll find a sculptor to do your likeness in marble."

"Unadorned?" Gregory teased.

"I should hope so," Patricia returned. "I'm trying to think whom you remind me of. All the men from my past have merged into a collage of faces and parts. The names have slipped my mind. If I didn't know better, I would swear you were a direct descendent of my beloved Edward—as rightfully you should be now that you're his grandson."

"It was a tiring trip, Mother," Susannah stated. "Can we freshen up and get settled before we continue our visit?"

"By all means. Marcia, you take your mother and Jim to their chambers. Stuart, give them a hand with the luggage and get them settled in." She clung to Gregory's hand. "You're not fatigued from the journey, are you, Gregory?"

"No, Grandmother. I would be pleased to stay with you for a while. I brought you a gift."

The others left the room. Ilene remained in the chair beside the window. Never had she been so greatly impressed by the appearance of a man as she was with Gregory's.

"What is it?" Patricia asked, as her old hands touched the brightly wrapped package.

"Guess."

"I'm too old for guessing games, Grandson," Patricia replied. "And I fear my fingers are too weak to undo the wrappings."

"Would you like me to do it for you, Mrs. Phenwick?" Ilene asked from a distance.

"I can do it for her," Gregory said, hardly glancing at the girl, whose appearance was obscured by the sunlight flowing in through the window.

"Thank you, Ilene," the old lady said, "but your assistance won't be necessary. Not when I have a handsome young man to help me."

"Ilene?" Gregory asked, looking back as he fumbled to remove the wrapping.

"Ilene is the girl hired to look after me. Joseph Ornby will not allow me to be alone," Patricia related. "Still she is great comfort and quite a bright girl. Come forward, Ilene, and meet my grandson. Gregory Phenwick, this is Ilene Dumphy. Miss Ilene Dumphy."

"Pleased to meet you," Gregory nodded without taking his attention from the package. "Here it is."

"A box?" asked Patricia.

"It is my pleasure to meet you, Mr. Phenwick," Ilene said.

"Thank you. There's something inside the box, Grandmother. I surely hope you didn't think I'd cart an empty box to you all the way from Paris." He opened it.

"Ah, I can tell by the bottle, it's perfume."

"It is the most magnificent scent of violets I could find," Gregory exclaimed. "Once I smelled it, I said this is for my grandmother."

"Violets?" questioned Patricia.

"Violets?" echoed Ilene.

"Of course, violets." Gregory removed the top from the bottle and put it to Patricia's nose. "Here, Miss Duffy, would you like a smell?"

"It's Dumphy," Patricia corrected. "But we all call her Ilene."

"Very well, Ilene, would you like to have a whiff?" Gregory asked, for the first time getting a good look at the girl.

"I had rather hoped that you would come with the scent of violets, Gregory," Patricia stated.

"I beg your pardon?" Gregory questioned once he was able to take his glance from the attractive girl on the other side of the bed.

"I said nothing important," Patricia comment-

181

ed. "I rarely do these days. It was only the babblings of an old lady approaching senility. I love the violet perfume. You couldn't have pleased me more with any gift, Gregory."

"Joanna said you would undoubtedly like it," Gregory remarked, finally taking his eyes from Ilene.

"So Joanna is in on this, too." Patricia smiled.

"I don't understand."

Stuart arrived at the door and announced that he would show Gregory to his room. After Gregory kissed his grandmother again, the two men left the room. Tears came to Patricia's eyes.

"I'm in need of a handkerchief, Ilene," Patricia said. "If you will just touch it to my eyes. They have become watery. He is such a beautiful man—like his sister." She rolled her eyes toward the girl. "Don't you find him handsome, Ilene?"

"Extremely. I mean—"

"Don't correct yourself. He *is* handsome."

"That must be very expensive perfume," Ilene commented. "I can still smell the aroma."

"So can I, Ilene, so can I." Patricia closed her eyes. "I will rest until they are settled."

Later that afternoon Ilene was given time to go about her chores, to take a recess from the room. Gregory had arrived to sit with his grandmother. She wanted to be alone with him.

Ilene held Gregory's attention as she left. When he turned back to Patricia, she was watching him, a soft smile on her lips.

"I've seen many a beautiful girl in my time," Gregory stated, "but none that has fascinated me as Ilene does. It's quite extraordinary. I confess I'm a bit overwhelmed."

"Isn't that interesting?" Patricia said, motioning for him to take the chair beside her bed. "Ilene has been my pet project these last few months. I have transformed her from a straggly immigrant girl into a lady of bearing and propriety. At least that's what I think I've done."

"She was your project? I say, whatever for?" questioned Gregory as he relaxed back into the chair.

"Because I'm convinced she is going to be a significant Phenwick woman."

"A Phenwick woman?" Gregory laughed. "Whatever gave you that notion?"

"Augusta." The old lady chuckled smugly. "Oh yes, I do believe Augusta Phenwick is still very much in evidence among her heirs."

"Augusta Phenwick has been dead and gone for at least half a century," Gregory commented, humor still in his voice.

"Dead, yes. Gone? Of that I'm not at all certain," Patricia related. "One of these days you must go down into the ballroom and stand before her picture. Who knows, she might speak to you."

"Speak to me? Oh, Grandmother, I say, you have gone a bit—"

"I think the word you're looking for is 'balmy.' It is, however, not the case in this instance. Have a look one day, and you might be amazed by your own reactions. I thought it was nonsense at one time. I learned differently." Patricia reached for him to take his hand. "Now tell me about yourself and what you've been up to all these years."

That evening after supper the family was gathered in the parlor. Nancy and Peter had joined them. It had been a delightful time of rem-

183

iniscing, with Susannah holding forth in her mother's place as the center of interest. Stella was with Patricia and Ilene had gone to her room in hopes of finding Moorduke.

"It is unfortunate we cannot all gather in Aunt Patricia's room," Peter Phenwick observed as he relaxed and sipped from a glass of sherry. He too had aged greatly, appeared tired and lacked his old interest in life. He was sitting next to Susannah, and she reached over and took his hand.

"My dear Peter," Susannah said, "it is curious enough that we of the older generation have to be amused by these young people; but to be with the oldest generation might be a bit too much. Still I forget that Nancy is so young."

Nancy was about to make a comment when the door to the parlor swung open and Gordon stood full force at the threshold. All attention turned to him.

"Well well, a happy family gathering," Gordon stated. "How interesting that I was not included among the guests!"

"Gordon!" Stuart rose and went to his brother. "We tried to reach you, but you were nowhere to be found."

"I've never known you to be a liar, Stuart," his brother returned, "so I must take your word." He entered the room. "Cousin Susannah—and Gregory. I'm sorry, I've forgotten this man's name."

"Jim Cornhill."

"Oh yes, Mr. Susannah Phenwick," Gordon sneered.

"Gordon! For goodness' sake, what's come over you?" demanded Stuart.

Gordon's eyes grew wide and his heavy eyebrows scowled. "I would have been disappointed if you were not all here. Surely my brother has told you how I've been over the years. Haven't you, Stuart?"

"We've not gotten around to mentioning you yet, Gordon," Stuart returned. "But from appearances, I'm certain little explanation is necessary."

"Oh no, Brother! I will explain," Gordon continued, pulling away from Stuart's hold. He charged toward Susannah. "I have been appointed by God Almighty to spread His holy word. You—all of you—I know about you—you are instruments of Satan! The angel of the Lord told me—came to me in a dream and said that I must go forth and save the sinning Phenwicks."

Gregory questioned, "I say, is he serious?"

"I'm perfectly serious!" Gordon charged. "I demand that you all get on your knees, confess your sins and accept Jesus Christ as your savior, or you shall all—every last one of you—burn in the eternal fires of hell!"

"Stuart, get him out of here!" Marcia cried. "I can't take any of that this evening."

"You cannot face the truth, you mean!" Gordon ranted.

"Gregory, give me a hand," Stuart called, grabbing for Gordon's arm.

Both Gregory and Jim were on their feet.

"Gordon, stop that this instant," Peter commanded, not rising from his seat.

"And who is that? My sinful grandfather? So it is! You should be ashamed of yourself, old man, for taking unto yourself a young wife. Wasn't the memory of my precious grandmother enough for you that you had to go out and find a Southern—"

"Enough, Gordon!" Stuart declared as he and Gregory pulled him from the room.

Gordon screamed as he was taken through the hallway and out the front door.

"Unhand me! Both of you!" Gordon insisted. "It was that Irish slut who turned you against me—you my own brother!"

"That is untrue, Gordon!" Stuart fired back.

"Is it?" Gordon raved. "She told you about me and that night in the church, didn't she?"

"Gordon," Stuart said firmly, "I want you to leave this instant. We will discuss whatever is on your mind at a time you are more rational."

"I know she did!" Gordon yelled. "Very well, the forces of Satan will be called upon you for turning against your own brother! Repent, for the day of salvation is at hand!"

Realizing that he was making no headway, Gordon glared at Stuart and Gregory, uttered words that seemed to be in a foreign tongue and dashed down the steps. He was still muttering, raising his Bible high in the air as he strode down the street, occasionally looking back.

"What has happened to Gordon?" asked Gregory after he disappeared from their view.

"Come into the library, Gregory," Stuart said. "I need something stronger than sherry after that."

After Stuart poured them each a glass of brandy and he took a healthy swallow, he turned to Gregory and put his hand to his shoulder. "I'm frightened, Gregory, frightened for my brother—and what he might do."

"I say, I can see where you would be, old fellow," Gregory commented. "What's come over the bloke since I was last here?"

"A more intensified case of religion than he previously had," Stuart explained. "Oh, it's been coming on progressively over the years. Let's finish our drinks and get back to the others. They will be concerned."

Gregory put his hand to Stuart's arm. "I can see you're deeply worried. Don't you want to talk about it?"

"Later—when the others have retired," Stuart said. "I'm terribly concerned—and I don't know what to do about it."

Gregory squeezed his shoulder and they went back to join the others.

CHAPTER NINETEEN

Ilene had wished for the appearance of Moorduke that night. But there was no evidence of the leprechaun. She had wanted to tell him about meeting Gregory Phenwick and the strange and wonderful reaction she had had to him. Instead of sharing her feelings, she created imaginary pictures and what seemed to be impossible dreams about the man. She had responded to the presence of other men, but none had affected her as queerly, yet in such a positive way, as Gregory.

Having heard the raucous disturbance made by Gordon and gone to the front of the house to observe his violent exit, she momentarily put aside her romantic speculations about Patricia Phenwick's grandson. Upon returning to her room, she found sleep difficult and wished she had someone with whom to share her thoughts.

The last lingering stars were in the sky the next morning when Ilene awakened. Whispering, she called to Moorduke, but received no response. More and more he had been staying away for longer periods of time; and when he did present himself, he was gloomy and despondent, speaking mainly of his desire to return to the glen at Carrickfergus and his boredom with Boston. Perhaps he had gotten the courage to make the sea voyage without her, had found a congenial sailor and become his mate for the trip. Impossible imaginings!

She was washed and dressed by the time the first pink of dawn lit the horizon. Wearing a soft green dress she had re-created from one given her by Marcia, she looked as fresh as a spring morning. Her long hair was brushed straight and gathered with a yellow ribbon. The dress had been designed originally to be daringly low-cut and Ilene had lowered it even more. She also had a yellow ribbon tied about her neck and another about her left wrist.

Quietly she left the third-floor room and tiptoed down to the kitchen, where she helped herself to fresh fruit and made a cup of tea. She carried the tea and fruit to the garden, where a small round table often served as her breakfast table. She had also brought along several crusts of old bread, with which she would feed the birds. Several robins and bluejays anticipated her morning sessions and waited for her arrival, brazenly going to eat from her hand.

Arriving at the table, Ilene discovered a small bouquet of violets waiting for her. "Moorduke," she said aloud, as she held the flowers to her nose and breathed deeply of their fragrance.

"Moorduke isn't the only one who presents you the violets, child," a voice seemed to say as if it were a whisper on the early morning breeze.

"Who's there?"

"It is unimportant who, Ilene." It sounded like a woman's voice.

"Do I know you?"

"I think not, yet you have seen my likeness. The violets are my assurance that you have been

chosen, Ilene. I need say no more." The voice disappeared like a fading sigh.

"But these violets are real." She smelled them again. "Moorduke?"

A bluejay swooped down and grabbed half a crust of bread from her. He dropped it. Soon three jays were arguing over the morsel. She watched as she finished her tea.

Gregory could not sleep late that morning. He was troubled by the situation he had observed with Gordon. He had gone for a long walk to sort his thoughts and attempt to find a solution. Ironically he found his thoughts vacillating from the problem with his cousin to singular speculations about the girl he had met the day before in his grandmother's room. Her face held a haunting memory for him. For some reason she was not just any girl, but someone special. Patricia had spoken in glowing terms about Ilene, boasting of her transformation. The old lady was also impressed that any person who could make such enormous changes in herself in such a short period of time surely had much to offer a man of importance. Patricia even had gone so far as to express that Ilene had the stuff from which Phenwick women were made. Had she planted thoughts in his mind? He would not put it past her.

As he returned to Edward House, Gregory could hear the chattering of bluejays from the back of the building. Certain no one but the servants would be up at this hour, he decided to go around and relax in the garden. Or was he being prodded into going in that direction by some unseen force? Why did an image of the portrait of Augusta flash into his mind? His expression turned into one of delight as he beheld Ilene amusing herself with the birds.

"May I interrupt your play?" he asked as he neared her.

"Oh, deary me!" she exclaimed. "You startled me."

"I'm sorry. I hadn't meant to. May I take a seat?"

"Please do, Mr. Phenwick," Ilene replied, her eyes feasting on the comely man who radiated a fantastic charisma. "Would you care for a peach? I brought two."

"Thank you, no. I have no appetite for food so early in the morning," Gregory replied.

"You are up early."

"The first night in Boston," Gregory laughed, "and a strange bed made it difficult for me to sleep any later. I actually was up before dawn—a practice that is not uncommon to me when I am on holiday." His eyes became so penetrating as he surveyed the pretty creature that she became uneasy and looked down, certain she was about to blush. "Violets?"

Ilene glanced up. "I suspect Moorduke—I mean a friend left them for me."

"A friend? Your leprechaun friend Grandmother told me about?" he asked.

"I suspect as much," Ilene said. "Oh dear, I didn't mean for Mrs. Phenwick to tell you about Moorduke. But it is suspicious. I mean usually when he presents me with violets no one else can see them."

"I can very definitely attest to the fact that they are quite visible to me." Gregory returned. "I say, you don't have another gentleman friend, do you?"

"Another? I don't really have any," Ilenē confessed, "unless you would consider Reverend Phenwick's interest in me in that category."

"Ah, so Gordon is pursuing you, is he?"

"We have had a run-in or two," Ilene said. "But I must say I don't find him altogether agreeable. He has such a way."

"After what I witnessed last night," Gregory inserted, "I can well see what you mean. But tell me about your leprechaun."

"Why would you be interested in such as him?"

"I'm British, you know," Gregory explained, "and I've encountered an Irishman or two who has told some farfetched tales about the little people. I have a rather good friend—a man—in London, who is Irish. He's an intelligent fellow, but he swears that he has had at least three encounters with fairies. At first I didn't take him seriously, but he is tremendously sincere in his belief. You'll have to meet him one day."

"How can I do that if he is in England?"

Gregory laughed, his face reddened slightly. "Perhaps we can arrange for you to make the trip."

"Oh, that would be ever so nice," Ilenē returned. "That way Moorduke could go back with me. He longs for Carrickfergus and the glen. He wants to be among his own kind. I guess he's tired of having a person all his own. Besides, he claims that he is concerned over his crocks of gold."

Gregory could not control his laughter. "My dearest Ilene, I should like to meet your leprechaun—not that I want his gold—but because he is so real to you."

"Moorduke isn't very sociable, Mr. Phenwick,

sar," she replied. "He's standoffish, if you know what I mean."

Patricia had awakened coughing. Stella, always alert to the old woman's slightest movement, went to the bed to lift her into a sitting position and pat her gently on the back.

"Are you all right, Mrs. Phenwick?" Stella questioned.

The coughing had ceased but she had a sharp pain in her chest. "I had a very vivid dream about my mother-in-law," she gasped. "Pull a chair to the window and help me to it. I want to gaze out into the garden. I must sit up for a while."

"It is very early in th' day for you to be doin' that, Mrs. Phenwick."

"Don't give me an argument, Stella," Patricia declared. "If I wish to sit up, that is what I want to do."

"Aye, Mrs. Phenwick." Stella scurried to push the large thronelike chair to the window. "I don't know what Dr. Ornby will say about this."

"I know what I will say if you disobey me," the old lady stated. "And that is that you are dismissed from your position. I need to sit up and get some fresh air. I'm suffocating."

Frightened, Stella managed to help Patricia to the chair by the window.

"Ah, this is better. Fresh air. The first few breaths are irritating to my lungs, but it is a needed change." Patricia sat back and relaxed. "Now it is easier. What a strange dream I was having. Augusta was so very real and her voice so distinct."

"Did it startle you, Mrs. Phenwick?"

"Startle? Yes. For a moment I thought she had

come to get me," the old lady stated. "I was not afraid. In fact, I rather hoped that that were the case. I am almost ready."

"Almost? Oh, Mrs. Phenwick, you should nay speak that way," Stella said, trembling. "Do you want me to send Dietrich for Dr. Ornby?"

Patricia chuckled softly. "I don't believe that will be necessary at this precise moment. Dr. Ornby will be around later this morning, as he usually is." She stared absently at the blue sky. "I still have another project I wish to see to completion—my final project. Push me forward toward the window so I can see down into the garden.

With effort, Stella managed to get the chair adjacent to the window. Patricia leaned to the side and looked down.

"Oh my! There are people sitting in my garden. Can you see who they are?"

Stella peered around the old lady, standing on tiptoe. "Why, 'tis Ilene and a young gentleman, Mrs. Phenwick."

"Which young gentleman?"

"I believe it is yer grandson."

"Gregory?" Patricia smiled. "And that other lady, standing beside them?"

"There is no other lady out there, Mrs. Phenwick. Only th' two o' them. Sure now, they're laughin'."

"What ails your eyes, girl? I distinctly see a lady standing. She is dressed in an old-fashioned way, and her hair—" Patricia hesitated. "Oh, I understand."

"How's that, Mrs. Phenwick?"

"Never mind, Shella. I am certain you do not see the lady."

Another pair of eyes was observing the young couple in the garden. They peered from behind a large yew bush at the front of the house so that the viewer was hidden from Gregory and Ilene. They stared for several minutes, widening as they reacted to the happiness of the young people.

"I have to admit I find you extremely interesting, Ilene," Gregory stated. "And I want to get to know you better."

"Why should you want to do that, Mr. Phenwick? I am only a serving girl."

"You may occupy that position now," he said, "but you have the bearing of a grand lady. If I didn't know otherwise, I would swear that you were a member of the aristocracy. I will also say I find you to be one of the most beautiful women I have ever seen."

"Go on with you," Ilene gushed.

"I'm perfectly serious," Gregory insisted. "If I make arrangements for you to have the day off, would you be kind enough to accompany me for a ride into the country? We can take a picnic along. Last time I was in Boston, Stuart showed me a delightful place for an outing away from the bustle of the city. My mother or Jim or even Marcia can sit with Grandmother."

"You want to take me on a picnic?" Ilene asked in amazement.

"We'll make a day of it."

"Why, Mr. Phenwick, I don't know what to say."

"Simply yes, that will be sufficient."

"But Mrs. Phenwick—Dr. Ornby—"

"Bits and pieces are coming together in my mind," Gregory stated. "Grandmother may well be in her final days, but her mind is sharp and she is still as scheming as ever. If I'm not mistaken, she will be more than delighted to give you the day off."

"I don't understand, Mr. Phenwick."

"Don't you? Good. Tuck those violets in your bosom and we'll go begin to make arrangements," Gregory instructed.

"Do you notice how almost overpowering the fragrance has become?" Ilene questioned. "I don't even have to hold them to my nose to smell them."

Gregory laughed. "Yes, my dear, the scent is almost overpowering. I will first speak with Marcia. My sister is very understanding. She will make the arrangements with Grandmother. This is to be a very special day for us, I can tell."

CHAPTER TWENTY

Gregory went to Marcia's room. Stuart was preparing himself for a day of business. Gregory quickly related his plans to his sister. She would be pleased to sit with Patricia.

"Are you certain about the violets, Gregory?" asked Marcia.

"As certain as you were when they happened to you," her brother replied. "I have never been as impressed in all my life with any woman as I am with Ilene."

"Don't be hasty," Marcia warned. "Ilene is a most unusual girl and she says some queer things."

"I know about the fairies and Moorduke," Gregory said. "Maybe I'll begin to believe in them, too."

"Gregory, be serious."

"I'm too giddy this morning to be serious about anything," Gregory replied. "I am on holiday, Sister dear, and I want to enjoy it as best I can."

A short while later Gregory helped Ilene into the shay. The picnic basket, blanket and cloth were in the back. He was like a playful boy, filled with anticipation and wonder.

"Sit close to me, Ilene," Gregory instructed. "I want to feel your nearness. It excites me."

"Excites you?" she questioned, feeling excitement within herself as well. She retied her bonnet so that it would remain in place as they rode.

"Lest you get any foolish ideas about me," Gregory explained, "I respect you, Ilene. And I want you to respect me, too. I have been trained to be a gentleman, and I have great moral admiration for ladies—especially for you."

The streets were bustling with activity as the shay drove through them. As they passed the Common, Ilene's attention was on the man beside her. Tim Dumphy, dressed in laborer's attire, stopped when he thought he recognized his sister.

"Hey! Ilene! D'you nay recognize yer brother anymore?" Tim called, turning about and running a short distance as if he thought he could catch up with the carriage. He flung his cap on the ground in disgust.

Ilene did happen to glance up as they went by the church where Gordon Phenwick was standing. He had looked up as if in response to Tim's voice. His eyes glared fury as he recognized Ilene with Gregory. She looked away from that fierce gaze, pretending she had not seen it. But those eyes seemed to be staring into her brain. She pushed closer to Gregory, which was next to impossible. Beside him she felt protected.

Soon they were out of the main section of town, traveling the road Stuart had directed Gregory to take. It was the way to Braintree, but they would turn off long before they reached that place.

They saw a slow-moving river and trees, open country and distant farms. Birds sang. Wild hares and squirrels scampered about in the open fields. The dirt lane was rough in places and the shay bounced and jostled them about. Greater and

greater excitement moved through Ilene. Anticipation. Happiness. She put the memory of Gordon's glaring eyes from her mind.

"It isn't often I get a holiday," Ilene explained
after they had found a colorful, isolated spot.
"But I enjoy working for Mrs. Phenwick. She has
taught me much. I've worked on my English and
even say final g's on words. You'd be amazed at
the patience she had with me. And at night I
would practice in my room. At first it was difficult,
but I believe I have conquered it."

Gregory held her hand. "I imagine you could
conquer anything you set out to accomplish,
Ilene."

"Why do you say that?"

"Because I believe that is the kind of person
you are."

"What a strange thing to say."

"Not at all. You are a very special person, I can
tell. Why, I should imagine if you found a man
you really wanted, you would know exactly how
to conquer him."

"Oh, Mr. Phenwick, you make me blush."

"It's a pretty blush, Ilene."

She looked down at their hands together. "And
are you a conqueror, too?"

"At times. I play many games. But I like obstacles and triumphing over them." Gregory lifted
her chin with his finger. "Have you ever been in
love, Ilene?"

"In love?" She tried to lower her head, but he
held it in place so that she had to gaze into his
eyes. "I have had a romantic fantasy or two about
different men. I think I would have found Dr.
Ornby easy to love—if he weren't already interested in my sister Sheila. He is a kind man."

"Aunt Patricia tells me that she has created you to be a Phenwick woman," Gregory stated, now letting her chin drift away from his finger.

The old lady has many a strange notion," Ilene responded.

"But she has determination," Gregory explained. "Marcia is a lot like her. Well, at the present time there are two available Phenwick men of marriageable age that I know of."

"There is Reverend Phenwick."

"He is one of the two."

"Oh."

"And you're holding the hand of the other," he said.

Impulsively Ilene attempted to pull her hand away, then relaxed. "Mr. Phenwick—"

Gregory released her hand. "Slowly, slowly. A wise don at school once told me to make haste slowly. I didn't comprehend what he meant at first—but I learned. I have never really been in love. I have had a few flings, romantic overtures. Nor have I led an altogether saintly life. I will not deny that I have had an affair or two. Girls, women are too eager to give themselves physically to me in hopes of becoming married into the Phenwick family. I've been aware of what they were up to. I don't say I haven't enjoyed such situations—I have for what they were. I never had a true desire to spend a lifetime with any of them."

"What was missing?" Ilene asked, a little disturbed that he should mention such things to her.

"In a word, love. A man can take pleasure from a woman without being in love with her," Gregory stated. "Just as I suppose a woman can do with a man. "But I detest having a woman submit to me when all she has in mind is ulterior motives, pretending pleasure, acting out a role. I've become leery, I confess."

"And do you think I'm playing a role, Mr. Phenwick?"

"Not in the least. You're different, Ilene. Even with your fantasies about fairies, there is a great sincerity in you. I feel that." Gregory took her hand again. "Don't mistake me, Ilene, I do find you physically desirable. I freely admit that. Still there is something about you that makes me want to know you better, to understand and fall in love with you."

"Fall in love?" Ilene stammered. "Oh, Mr. Phenwick, why ever would you want to do that?"

"Because you are lovable and worthy of respect," Gregory said sincerely. "With your permission, I would like to kiss you. Perhaps you then would begin to generate a little interest in me."

"A little interest?" Ilene smiled sweetly. She already had more than a little. "Then you may kiss me if you like."

He took her in his arms, stared deeply into her eyes before he put his lips to hers. There was no denying the excitement that flooded through her or the lovely reaction she was experiencing.

"Can you take a little interest in me, Ilene?"

"I believe more than a little interest, Mr. Phenwick."

They kissed again.

Peter and Nancy Phenwick arranged to have a dinner party that evening for their relatives from England. Naturally Stuart and Marcia were also invited. Nancy was unaware of the developments between Gregory and Ilene and, to balance her table, she invited a socialite friend, Sylvia Whitmore, to make an eighth at the table. While their four sons were permitted to visit with the guests, they were not to sit in the dining room with the adults. Thadius, the eldest, was thirteen and becoming quite a little gentleman. John, twelve, was also maturing. But the two younger boys, Paul and Daniel, were still childishly immature.

Sylvia Whitmore was an attractive lady with bright red hair. Her sophisticated manners and proper ways were well displayed. Still there was no mistaking that she found Gregory Phenwick to be an attractive man. Any woman of breeding and ambition would be honored to marry into the Phenwick family—and that was the attitude she projected.

It was a happy occasion with Peter and Susannah dominating the conversation with reminiscences of their youthful days in Boston and members of the illustrious Phenwick family who lived during that time. Marcia picked up additional information she could include in the history of the family on which she had collaborated with Patricia. She realized there were many other aspects about the clan that should be in the book. As a result she planned to spend time with Susannah and Peter to get their particular versions.

Gregory attempted to be congenial toward Sylvia Whitmore, but his thoughts were with Ilene. He was polite but basically indifferent toward the lady. In fact, as far as the others were concerned he was strangely abstract that evening.

At the end of the meal, Stuart offered Gregory a cigar and suggested they take a short stroll while they smoked so as not to disturb the others with the effluvia of tobacco. Jim Cornhill was content to join Peter in the study for a gentlemanly visit while the ladies adjourned to the parlor for sherry and demitasse. Sylvia realized she made no particularly lasting impression on Gregory, although she admitted to Nancy that she found him extremely attractive.

"Something troubling you, Gregory?" asked Stuart as they walked beneath the heavy-leafed trees.

"Why do you ask?"

"You seemed remarkably quiet this evening at dinner."

"It was your grandfather's and mother's show, as Joanna would say," Gregory returned. "Besides, I admit my thoughts were elsewhere."

"I'm concerned this evening," Stuart admitted. "I know you didn't ask, but I'll tell you. I tried to see Gordon today for a rational conversation. That was impossible. He acted as if he hardly knew me. I later spoke with Joe Ornby. And Joe said he was unable to make any headway with getting to Gordon. I'm worried. I finally stopped in and saw Cousin Daniel Ornby—he's the attorney, you know. Daniel is upset with Gordon. It seems he has been handling some business matters for him. Gordon has accumulated quite a bit of property—which is none of my business—but his reason for doing so seems somewhat questionable. Dan didn't explain what he meant by that. However, he did say that Gordon had been to see him yesterday and asked to arrange for him to get several thousand dollars in cash. Dan was able to negotiate a loan on property owned by Gordon. Then my brother went into a bizarre tantrum— that's what Dan called it. He almost became violent because Dan had been unable to arrange for the specified amount of money Gordon wanted."

"Gordon's become irrational," Gregory remarked. "I noticed that last night."

"Dan questions his sanity. Frankly, I believe Joe has doubts about his mind, too," Stuart said. "It worries me. He is my brother."

"But what do you do about him? Is that the problem?"

"Yes. Dan says there's nothing that can legally be done unless he actually does something against the law," Stuart continued. "I mean he would have to do something pretty drastic for us to take legal measures to have him—well—confined."

"But he uses his religious dealings as a cover," Gregory commented. "Other preachers are as zealous as he is. We even have them in London. You don't believe Gordon might become violent, do you?"

"He was always fairly gentle as a child," Stuart replied. "Yet there is no doubt he has some violence in his nature. I suppose we just have to wait and see what happens next."

Gregory put his hand to his cousin's shoulder. "If there's anything I can do—"

"We can only wait and see how this thing turns out." Stuart puffed hard on the cigar. "And what's on your mind tonight?"

"Love."

"Love?" Stuart chuckled and nearly choked on the smoke.

"My question is, how does one know when he is in love?"

Stuart thought a moment. "I suppose when the right person comes along, you instinctively know. I knew I loved Marcia long before she realized she loved me. I don't think all people—perhaps not many people—fall in love with each other at the same time."

"I've just met her, but I know," Gregory stated.

"I beg your pardon?"

"Ilene Dumphy. I've known many ladies, even in intimate situations, but I never felt for any of them as I feel for Ilene," Gregory confessed. "Maybe Grandmother conditioned me—but whatever she did seems to have worked. I don't blame Grandmother for my feelings. I do have a wonderful and confusing attitude toward Ilene—which I can only believe to be love."

Stuart stopped beneath a lamppost. "The one ingredient I believe that most determines the truth of love is time."

"Yes, I know, make haste slowly. But you understand."

"I do understand, Gregory. And I believe you couldn't find a nicer person than Ilene."

"I was hoping you would say that."

"Maybe we should get back to the others."

Stuart and Gregory returned, mostly walking in silence as each became absorbed in his own thoughts.

CHAPTER TWENTY-ONE

The note had been delivered by messenger that afternoon. Dietrich had received it. Since it was not for one of the Phenwicks, he carelessly left it in the kitchen on the counter. It was not until he had had his supper in that room that his attention was attracted to the envelope. Leisurely he climbed the stairs to the third floor to deliver it to Ilene.

Ilene was in a dreamy mood, staring distantly out the window into the garden below and remembering her early morning meeting with Gregory. So much had happened that day and she was in a glowing mood.

Dietrich simply mentioned that a note had come for her and left the room.

"'My sister Ilene'," she read aloud, "'I must see you tonight at eight o'clock at 1743 Elm Street. Since this meeting concerns your family, you are to come alone. No outsiders are wanted. Be there. Your brother Tim'." The writing was unmistakably the scribbling of her brother. Some of the words she had difficulty making out. Tim wrote with a downward-sloping scrawl with imperfectly formed letters. It was the writing his mother had taught him, but he had been a poor student.

Seven o'clock. Ilene heard the chimes ringing

from the second floor and the echo from another clock on the first floor. A meeting that concerned her family? Immediately she thought of her father and his failing health. A sense of urgency came over her. She looked to find Moorduke, even calling to him; but he did not put in an appearance.

Ilene went to find Dietrich and asked if he knew where 1743 Elm Street was. The man was vague. The serving girl, Mattie, knew approximately where it was, but explained that it would be a tiring walk from Edward House. Besides, it was not in a very respectable neighborhood for a young woman to enter that hour of the approaching night.

Going from the kitchen to the second floor, Ilene rapped at the door to Patricia's room.

"There are family problems, Mrs. Phenwick," she announced, flapping the note toward the old woman. "My brother wishes to see me by eight o'clock at 1743 Elm Street. Dietrich has given me instructions to get there, but it is quite a distance. Tim, my brother, makes it sound urgently important."

Patricia was groggy and ready for sleep. "The carriages are gone. If you ride, there should be a horse or two in the stable. I don't know how reliable they are."

"I can ride," Ilene stated, not bothering to mention that she rode astraddle as her brothers had taught her. "May I take a horse?"

"If you promise to be careful," Patricia sighed. She did not much care about what was happening, but she could sense the urgency in Ilene's voice. "What was the address again?"

"1743 Elm Street."

"1743 Elm Street," Patricia repeated and

closed her eyes. "I will see you in the morning,
Ilene. You can tell me all about your family." Her
eyes opened. "I would also like to hear what your
day was like today. But that can wait. Goodnight." Ilene was out of the room before Patricia's
eyes opened again. "1743 Elm Street. My word,
she can't be thinking of going into that district
this hour of the night. Well, if it's family matters—"

"What is it, Mrs. Phenwick?" asked Stella.

"Nothing important," the old lady moaned. "I
can't think now. I just want to go to sleep. Don't
disturb me, Stella."

The stableman saddled an older mare, one who
had seen better days. The black horse was led out
of the carriage house and Ilene was helped up.
She was wearing an older, durable dress, which
was gray and white. She rarely wore it because it
was plain and lacked character. It would do for
meeting her brother.

The address was a good four miles from Edward House. Twice Ilene became confused by the
directions and had to ask for assistance. As she
approached the neighborhood and the 1600
block on Elm Street, a feeling of apprehension
came over her. The buildings were very old, many
of the houses boarded up. Nobody was on the
street and only an occasional streetlamp was lit.

The house at 1743 Elm Street was ancient. A
wooden, paintless structure, it was three stories
high. Most of the windows were boarded over. A
horse and cart were tied at the post outside. Otherwise there was no indication that anyone was
there.

She dismounted and tied the horse. Only because she knew her brother so well and that he

liked such out-of-the-way places did she consider investigating further. Tim was always involved with the unusual, without any pretense of grandeur or show. Somehow this ragged-looking old house seemed to be the type of place he might choose.

One of the steps was loose and slapped when she mounted it. The floorboards of the porch were old and rotting. They creaked eerily with every step she took. The porch ceiling echoed in response and she heard rustling noises in the rafters as if birds were perched there and had been disturbed by her arrival. Did bats inhabit such places? She was afraid to even consider that possibility, although the thought persisted in her consciousness.

The outer door was off one hinge and was gaping slightly. She pushed it aside. Finding no knocker, she put her curled fist to the inner door in an attempt to knock. The force of her hand pushed the door open.

A single lamp was lit on an old table. A foul, musty smell rushed at her. Because she observed a note on the table, Ilene trembling went toward it.

"Ilene—come to the second floor." Was the scribbling that of her brother?

As she pondered over the soiled piece of paper and glanced up the foreboding flight of dark stairs, the front door closed and the lock turned, as if a key had been applied to it from the outside.

Hurriedly Ilene went back to the door. It was solidly closed. When she tried to force it, the entire wall seemed to creak in response.

"Oh me God! B'gorra, I've been locked in," she

said, reverting to her Irish dialect. "'Tis nay a funny thing, Tim Dumphy, what you've done." She turned around and called into the room. "I do nay care for yer prank, Tim Dumphy!"

Her voice echoed gloomily back at her. She raised a foot, but held it a moment before lowering it. Then a streak of anger went through her and she was determined to find her brother and get the matter clarified once and for all. Possessed with a surge of annoyed urgency mixed with courage, she went to the table and got the lamp. Moments later she was halfway up the stairs before she was aware of the trembling steps and wondered if they would hold her weight as she made it to the second floor.

All doors were closed and apparently locked, except one. Not only was it slightly ajar, but a faint glow of flickering light came from it. The foul stench she had smelled below was more noticeable as she neared the open door.

Pushing the door inward, Ilene beheld a particularly large room. Crude benches were lined in two rows around three sides of it. A large table was in the center, upon which a single black candle was burning. Over it a cross was hanging, but it was upside down. A large circle was painted on the floor and within was a second circle. A five-pointed star stood out in the inner circle and around it were painted strange figures. The star, too, looked as if it were upside down, with two points of it aimed toward the table. Another star was on the back wall, and it too was reversed, the two points projecting upward like an animal's horns. Around the table were crusty, brownish-looking spots of various sizes. They resembled dried blood. The table itself had a few similar spots and was gouged with several scars.

Ilene experienced a terrible reaction as she stood in the room. A sick feeling came over her and she felt as if she were going to be nauseous. Finding her voice, she called her brother's name. There was no answer. But as she listened carefully, she thought she heard a scramble of whispered syllables coming from somewhere in the distance. She stared up at the slightly swinging, inverted cross and beyond to the ceiling from which it was suspended. Was the sound coming from the floor above?

Clutching the lamp, using both hands because she was trembling so, she stealthily left the room, taking the door through which she had entered rather than one of the two doors at the rear of the room which were either side of the painted pentagram on the wall.

The stairs to the third floor were as precarious as those she had trod to the second floor. An even more profound feeling of apprehension moved through her as she climbed, each step creaking as if in pain as she touched it. For a fleeting moment she thought that the old house could well have been a lavish mansion at one time. But the era of its elegant glory was past.

Several closed doors led off from the third-floor hallway. No light came from anywhere. As she pondered which of the doors she should try first, one at the end of the hallway slowly opened. She could not find her voice to call Tim. Standing frozen for a moment, her impulse was to go back downstairs, to retreat. But to where? The front door was solidly locked. Now anger and impatience came over her and she was determined to get to the bottom of this foolish prank that Tim had engineered.

The door pulled wider into the room as she approached it. She had to use both hands to keep the lamp from slipping from her hands. The light danced eerie shadows over the wall.

As she entered the room, the door was pushed closed behind her and she was aware of a group of several robed and hooded people standing about her. Their faces were covered with shadows and masks. A hand snatched the lamp from her, while two other hands on each side grabbed her arms and pulled her forward into the room.

Black coverings were pulled from four lanterns at the end of the room and she cringed with horror as she stared at the most frightening image she had ever seen. It looked part man and part animal. The head was that of a large goat, with leering red eyes and horns that were exaggerated. The upper body was covered with a fleece jerkin, the lower body and legs were exposed. He was seated on a throne on a dais. As he beckoned her forward, he rose. Corpulent legs, sturdy, bare feet. She avoided looking at the rest of him.

Hoods were pushed back on several of the people, revealing the masked faces of old women. The men appeared to be deformed. Both men and women wore nothing beneath their cloaks and the bodies that were exposed were twisted, withered and ugly. Ilene was repulsed and tried not to see the dreadful creatures.

"Thou standeth in the presence of Satan!" a man's quivering voice cried.

The cloaked creatures crept around her in a circle as if each were examining her. Ilene could not see their eyes in the black masks, but she could feel them scrutinizing her. Then the circle broke and the individual in the goathead mask approached her. She kept her gaze over his shoulder, not daring to look him in the face or at any other part.

"Ilene Dumphy," the voice said, muffled behind the mask, "thou hast been chosen to be the bride of Satan! Take her away and prepare her in the black bridal gown. The ceremonies shall commence! Prepare thyself for me!"

"Who or what are you?" Ilene asked.

The Satanic creature turned about and strode back to the throne. His large backside, especially the unexposed part, moved with a self-assured air. There was no mistaking what his ultimate intentions were for her. In that fleeting moment the thought occurred to her that Satan should be more svelte with sinewy muscles. Where had she gotten that notion?

The old women had hold of Ilene with clawing strength. They ripped at her dress.

"Why are you doing this to me?" Ilene called, turning back as she felt the garments being peeled from her.

"Because thou art one of us," the man's voice called from behind the goathead mask. "Thou hast the power to call forth incubi. Take her to the altar whilst I prepare myself! Go!"

In the torment of her confusion, Ilene could not comprehend what he meant, indeed if his words had meaning at all. "Where is my brother?"

The old women cackled menacingly and pushed her from the room. She was taken to a room on the second floor, where the women removed the rest of her clothing and tugged her into diaphanous black gown, more like flimsy sleeping apparel, she thought, than a wedding gown. Her face was covered with a black veil.

CHAPTER TWENTY-TWO

By the time Gregory and Stuart returned from their walk, the former had put his thoughts into order. He stopped before going up the front steps.

"What is it?" asked Stuart.

"Can we stay out a few minutes longer?" Gregory asked. "There is something more I must tell you."

"Another confession?"

"I know I must seem childlike to you, Stuart."

"On the contrary, you appear to be a well-rounded man, who knows what he wants," Stuart commented.

"Businesswise I know perfectly well what I want," Gregory explained. "But it is my personal life that is confusion. I say, in London I'm known to be quite a man-about-town. Everyone knows me for my wealth and position. I'm a member of a very exclusive club. Between my mother and Joanna, Joshua and Olivia, I am a social attraction. I have my choice of women—and there have been quite a few. But I fear them."

"You fear women?"

"Not in general," Gregory replied, "but those in London to whom I'm introduced for one reason or another. Most of them are out to snag me for what I am, not who I am."

"I beg your pardon."

"They want to entice me into marriage because I am an eligible Phenwick man," Gregory said. "Mother is still a famous concert pianist. Joanna is acclaimed as leading actress on the London stage. Even Olivia, who has returned to acting, is well-known. Joshua has long fought off the advances of designing women. We both retreat to the club to escape the designs of certain persons. He has an out, he's happily married to Olivia. Still, while she is at the theater every night, Joshua doesn't enjoy strictly the company of men friends, nor does he stay at home with his children all the time."

"Sounds like Uncle Joshua is quite a playboy, too," Stuart commented. "He always knew his way around well."

"But he isn't all that promiscuous—as I'm not," Gregory explained. "Debauchery becomes old after a while—and meaningless."

"Fortunately I never permitted myself to get into that sort of a routine," Stuart remarked with a slight laugh. "Nor have I ever had the desire. Still this is Boston, proper and sedate. You live in notorious London. There's a difference."

"Agreed. You see, Stuart, one has to have certain values in life, or it begins to lose its importance," Gregory stated. "I do have moral values. I realize that more and more. True, I've had my flings, tried many diverse things and experiences, none of which I am particularly proud of. But I've done all that, don't you know. Now I'm ready to settle down, to have a family."

"And you believe Ilene—?"

"I know. I instinctively know," Gregory exclaimed. "While she is intelligent, she is simple in her tastes—she's not been spoiled. Fact is, it may take her a while to adjust to such an opulent way of life. Yet I feel she will always maintain a certain degree of innocence I find appealing."

"Have you discussed all this with Susannah?" Stuart asked, finding it difficult to keep his mind on Gregory's problem when he was so deeply concerned about Gordon.

"Not yet. But I will. I'll give myself another few days to get to know Ilene better," Gregory said, "then I'll mention it to Mother."

"You've made up your mind then?"

"I believe I have," Gregory said. "I'll take things slowly until I'm absolutely certain."

"We had best get inside," Stuart stated. "The others will think we have deserted them. I don't want to cause Marcia any needless worry in her condition."

The two men went into the house and joined the others.

A little while earlier Sheila Dumphy cleaned and straightened up after the dinner meal. It was meager fare. Sean Dumphy, as usual, retired immediately after supper. He was not well. Sheila looked in on her father, but he was sound asleep.

Sheila had hoped that Dr. Joseph Ornby would come to visit that evening. She was very fond of the man. He came often to see her. If only there was someone to look after the younger Dumphy children. Frustrated and discontent, she could see no way in the immediate future for her to change her status. The younger children could be little solace to her, and she would not impose on either Molly or Ilene.

The sound of an arriving carriage aroused Sheila's hopes. Instead of seeing Dr. Joseph when she went to the door, she saw her brother Tim throwing the reins to Mickey to tie the horse. He dashed into the shanty and picked Sheila up.

"What is th' meanin' o' this, Tim Dumphy?" Sheila asked. "Put me down this very minute. Are you drunk?"

"Aye, Sheila, me love," Tim exclaimed. "I'm drunk with power. 'Tis a windfall I've had."

"What are you goin' on about?"

Tim pulled a fistful of currency from his pocket and brushed it under his sister's nose. "Would you gi' a look at this?"

"Glory be! What've you got there, Tim?"

"What does it look like, lass?"

"Money."

"B'gorra, yer eyes ain't deceivin' ya none," Tim declared. "I've got this and another pocketful, I have."

"Where did you git it?"

"Maybe you're a-thinkin' I robbed some'un, ain't ya? Well, 'tain't so," Tim stated. "I've got me more put away. And if'n I play me cards right, there's plenty more where this cum frum."

"Tim, you've got me dizzy flashin' that money about," Sheila said, catching his hand.

"Here. It's for you," Tim explained.

"Is it clean money, Tim?"

"Aye, they're practically new hundred-dollar bills, they are."

"That's nay what I meant," Sheila returned.

"Oh, I worked for th' money, if'n that's what you mean," Tim said, laughing. "Since you'll nay see any o' th' b'ys what I want ya to meet—"

"Th' b'ys you want me to meet! You mean th' rowdies, don't ya?"

"Aye, Sheila, 'tis nay nice to say unkind things

about me friends," Tim scolded. "And here I am, givin' ya money like it growed on trees."

"What *did* you do to git this money, Tim?"

"I took up writin', I did." He blew on his finger-tips and rubbed them against his blouse.

"Writin'? Go on with ya, you're full o' m'larky, you are!"

"Ya needn't scoff at me none, lass, 'tis th' truth I'm a-tellin' ya."

"I'll be thankin' you to explain what you mean, Timothy Dumphy," Sheila fired. "You don't know how to write one word frum th' next."

"I do, if'n I copy 'em," Tim declared. "And I'll thank ya to know you're holdin' Phenwick money, that's what ya are. And I niver had to sit with some old dyin' lady to git it either."

"Tell me exactly how you got this money, Tim. I have a queer feelin' when you speak o' it," Sheila said. "And I don't much like th' look in yer face."

"Well, it seems there's a Phenwick gent what's taken a fancy to our sister."

"Which one?"

"Ilene."

"I mean which gent?"

"Hauld yer harses, lass," Tim stated. "Did ya count th' money?"

"Nay, and I will nay do so until I git to th' bottom o' this," Sheila expressed, her face red with anger.

Tim knew he could taunt his sister only just so long. With minute detail he explained how he was approached by a Phenwick gentleman, who offered him a handsome sum to write a note to his sister asking her to meet her brother—not him—at an address on Elm Street.

Sheila listened, her anger becoming mixed with fear. After Tim finished his lengthy explanation, she said, "You'll take me this instant to th' home o' Dr. Ornby. He's told me o' that man! And what you've done may have put Ilene into a grave situation."

"I do nay understand," Tim returned.

"I'll tell ya on th' way. 'Tis eight o'clock now or after," Sheila stated. "We've nay a second to waste. D'you remember th' number o' th' house what was in th' note?"

"'Twas 17 somethin'," Tim said. "I'll try to remember it."

Joseph had been called to the bedside of old Myrtle Belcher, a woman who was in great pain and seemed to be in the slow process of dying. Mrs. Belcher lived in a small cottage on the outskirts of the city. When Hiram Belcher was alive they had had a large farm in the country. Myrtle had sold much of her land as the city expanded, retaining only an acre of land that surrounded the ancient farmhouse.

Always a peculiar lady, Myrtle Belcher was considered by her neighbors to be strange, different. Never an attractive person, time had gnarled her features, twisted her bones and caused her to have a grotesque shape. Her hooked nose and toothless mouth gave her face a frightening appearance. Heavy brows made it seem she was perpetually scowling.

Dr. Joseph Ornby had made several visits to the old lady, called at the request of one of her concerned neighbors. On his first visit Myrtle had made it perfectly plain that she did not put any stock in doctors because they overlooked the true remedies of nature. Furthermore they looked upon themselves as some sort of Christian demagogues and she was not sympathetic to such a philosophy. However, after he was able to relieve some of the severe pain Myrtle had been experiencing, she softened her opinion of the man and allowed him to return. Finally she sent in desperation for him to come. And he did.

"You don't need to tell me, Doctor," the toothless woman mumbled. "I know I'm dyin'. It's no surprise at my time of life. Isn't there somethin' you could give me to make the end come sooner?"

"No, Mrs. Belcher," Joseph said, "that would be unethical."

"If I could only get out in the woods," Myrtle moaned, "I'd find me the right roots and herbs to concoct me a precious poison. But I no longer have the strength. I can barely rise from my bed. Nightly I call upon Satan to come and deliver me."

"Upon Satan?" Joseph questioned, after examining her and giving her a sedative. "You don't pray to God?"

"Never!" Myrtle scorned. "I have long worshiped the devil. My late husband, Hiram, never approved. At least he never professed to be a Christian. Does it repel you that I speak of such things?"

"Not repel, Mrs. Belcher," Joseph answered. "It arouses my curiosity, however."

"Do you innocently believe like so many of the others," Myrtle questioned, "that worship of Satan no longer exists?" She cackled, then fell into coughing. "It does. Right here in the holy city of Boston. Even the street preachers who stand on the corners shaking tambourines are in a sense praisin' Satan simply by recognizin' his existencē. Fact is, there are those with pious attitudes who are two-faced and, while preachin' good, practice evil in secret."

"Do you belong to a Satanist cult, Mrs. Belcher?"

"I used to," the old lady sighed. "Here back about three months ago some boy shot my black cat. It was an omen. I knew I would fall to bed and never get out of it alive. But I do not fear death, Dr. Ornby. I'm rather lookin' forward to the debauchery of hell. I haven't been to a good orgy in a long time."

"You have actually participated in Satanist rites?"

"I would just as soon be burnt at the stake as suffer the physical pain I am sufferin'," Myrtle allowed, "So I freely admit that I am a witch. The children were right when they called me such when I used to go out. I would always raise my cane and shoo them away. But inwardly I liked the recognition. Are you appalled, young doctor?"

Believing the woman to be delirious and not in her right mind, Joseph tried his best to comfort her. "No, I'm not appalled. I have an open mind."

"Ornby? Your father was an attorney, wasn't he?" asked Myrtle as she stared dimly into the man's face.

"My father is a physician," Joseph corrected. "My Uncle Daniel is an attorney, as was my grandfather."

"Andrew Ornby?"

"That was my grandfather."

"Ah, then you are related to the high and mighty Phenwicks, aren't you?"

"Yes."

Myrtle cackled contemptuously. "Did you know that Lillian Phenwick was a client of mine?"

"Lillian? The wife of Augustus Phenwick?"

"The same. She used to come to me to make voodoo dolls," the woman confessed. "And they worked. She was one of those two-way people. One side of her embraced Christianity while the other paid homage to Satan. Not unlike—" She stopped and cast him a suspicious glance. "Not unlike others I know. But Lillian Phenwick failed me. She didn't keep her part of the bargain, hence the curse was reversed and she was destroyed."

"Failed you?"

"She had promised to get the books for me," Myrtle said slowly and with difficulty. "I didn't want them to be printed so that our secrets would be known to any who chanced upon them."

"The books?"

"The books written by Rosea Hackleby. When I was younger I innocently gave the old lady information I know she recorded," Myrtle Belcher related. "Now there are at least a hundred copies of the books."

Uneasily, Joseph said, "I believe I have done all I can do for you this evening, Mrs. Belcher. If you like, I will come again tomorrow."

"I have a premonition you won't need to bother tomorrow, Dr. Ornby," the old woman sighed. "I only wish you had a cup of hemlock to offer me now." She made a sound somewhere between a cough and a chuckle. Her body shook as she reached a withered hand toward the doctor. "Wait. I think you would do well to hear me out. I have paid you nothin', nor will you receive anything after I'm gone—still you have come to call on me as if I were one of your wealthy patients. I appreciate that. You have eased my pain somewhat."

"I must get back to the city."

"Another sick one?"

"No. But I have put in a long day," Joseph explained.

"There is a coven tonight," Myrtle said as if she had plucked the thought out of the blue. "I would have liked to have gone for one last feast with Satan."

Now convinced she was delirious, Joseph put his hand to her forehead. She caught his wrists with twiglike fingers.

"Satan is taking a virgin bride," Myrtle mumbled. "The moon will be full shortly after nine-thirty. The young innocent will be taken by the warlock. And if she lives to tell about it, she will have become a convert to the devil."

"This is all very interesting, Mrs. Belcher, but I really must—"

"Do the initials I.D. mean anything to you?"

Joseph eased his hand from her tenacious grip. "No, nothing."

Myrtle laughed. "They might stand for *insane deed*, or—let me think—Irish damsel—or they might even be the girl's initials."

"*Irish damsel*?" Joseph questioned. Then he thought of someone who possessed those initials. "What is it, Mrs. Belcher? What are you trying to tell me?"

"There is a coven, Dr. Ornby, tonight. It has already begun." Myrtle moved as if in discomfort. "Only because of your kindness to me do I mention this to you. I don't believe you will be able to prevent the initiation."

"Where is this—this coven to take place?"

"Ah, I've whetted your interest."

"If those initials stand for whom I'm thinking—"

"Give me an extra-heavy dose of sedative—a strong dose, Doctor," Myrtle bargained, "a very strong dose." She clutched her withered breast and cried out in agony. From her tortured expression, a grim grin came to her toothless mouth. "Perhaps it is too late. I won't need the sedative after all. The pain is gone now—completely gone. Well well. Elm."

"Elm?"

"It's on Elm," Myrtle gasped. "17—"

"17—?"

"43. That was a good year for witches, I believe." She sighed. Her eyes were sightless as they seemed to be directed toward Joseph's face.

He reached for a pulse. There was none. After checking other signs, he closed her eyes and drew the cover up over her face.

As a strange urgency seemed to come over him, Joseph gazed around the dirty, disheveled room. In the corner on the wall in heavy shadows was an inverted cross. He had read enough of *The Mysteries of Rosea Hackleby* to know that that symbol indicated Myrtle Belcher indeed was an advocate of the devil. Why had she told him what she had? Was it somehow her meager way of repaying his kindness?

Gathering his things, Joseph quickly left the house, firmly closing the door behind him. He checked his pocket watch. Eight-twenty. It was a twenty-minute drive back to his home. Moments later he was in the shay and urging the horse at full speed toward the center of Boston.

CHAPTER TWENTY-THREE

After being dressed in the black diaphanous gown and the black veil, Ilene was tied to a chair in a small room across from the room where she had seen the hideous altar to Satan. In the distance she could hear a church bell ringing the half hour. What time was it? Eight-thirty? Everything had happened so rapidly that she had lost any concept of time. Trembling with fear, she tugged at the ropes which bound her. The pain cutting into her flesh was excruciating.

"Moorduke! Where are you now that I need you most?" she called. The small room made her voice sound dull.

The windows were boarded over and she sat in stark darkness. A vile odor hung in the room, like something rotting.

"Moorduke, I know why you won't appear to me," Ilene stated, half whimpering. "You're angry at me, aren't you? You think that I've fallen in love with a mortal man, don't you? You're jealous. I know you and the way you think. But if you allow this terrible thing to happen to me, I will know that you were a malicious imp all along." She sobbed. "You want me for yourself. I have been aware of that for a long time. But that is not practical, Moorduke. You're not a mortal and I am. We can always be friends, Moorduke, but you must realize that I need the fulfillment of love for a human man. I always knew you would desert me when I found such a man. Why don't you appear to me? Make yourself visible!"

The room was deathly quiet. The only sounds she could hear were in the distance.

"Moorduke, I was hoping you would be happy for me," Ilene continued, as if speaking to an imaginary person made her feel less alone. "I realize that I do love Mr. Phenwick. I have a different feeling for him than I had for Dr. Ornby or any other man I have ever known. I can't explain how it is different, but I know it is true. I want you to understand and be happy for me, Moorduke. But you're not happy, are you? You're jealous and in a fit of rage. Well, go on with you, I'll see myself through this."

She heard the sound of the key being turned in the lock. The door opened. Only a tiny bit of light came through the opening as two shrouded figures crept into the room.

The veil was raised from Ilene's face and she felt a cup placed to her lips.

"Here. Drink this," a crackling voice ordered.

Ilene could not tell whether it was a man or a woman. "What is it?"

"Ask no questions. Drink."

The other voice said, "It will help prepare you for the wedding."

"I don't want it," Ilene objected.

"But you will drink it nevertheless," the first voice said. "It was mixed while we were standing in the magic pentagram. It will add to your pleasure during the ritual."

"Take it away!"

"Pry her mouth, Gertrude."

"She bit me!"

"Give her a slap, then get a good grip."

The slap was resounding. Ilene screamed with the sting. A moment later two powerful hands, one on her chin and another on her nose, pulled in opposite directions. Ilene resisted as best she could, but the horrid-tasting concoction was poured into her mouth. Her jaw slammed closed. A hand massaged her throat to make her swallow, while the other two hands kept her mouth and nose closed. Ilene fought for breath and choked as the liquid ran down into her throat.

"Is it swallowed?"

"Moorduke, for God's sake, help me!"

"It's swallowed."

"Come."

The two figures moved from the room, closed and locked the door behind them.

Ilene wanted to gag from the awful taste. If only she had a hand free she could force herself to regurgitate. The veil was back down over her face as she felt a dizzying sensation come to her head. Then her body became fiery hot and tingled from head to toe. That prickly heat continued until she squirmed about as much as she could as if she were attempting to rid herself of a terrible itching. Her head swung from side to side in a rolling movement that only seemed to make her thoughts fuzzy and distorted. Slumping forward, she felt she was being consumed by fire. Then a sensation of uncontrollable passion possessed her that was sheer agony.

"Oh God! If there is a God, or whatever Power controls the universe, help me!" she screamed.

Her chin fell to her chest again as her head seemed to light up inside.

"I will resist!" she kept telling herself, muttering it over and over again.

No sense of time in that drugged state—Ilene imagined she was in a hollow, timeless tunnel as the desire for sensual release overwhelmingly increased. Her pulse was racing and she had difficulty catching her breath.

"Breathe deeply ... slowly," she told herself. With great effort she managed to take ten large breaths. Then her head rolled to the side and she sat in a heavy fog.

In that timeless state, Ilene perceived she had been tied to the chair for an eternity.

"Moorduke?"

Was it her imagination or did she suddenly become aware of the scent of violets? With effort she raised her head and breathed in deeply. Yes, the scent of violets! Had Moorduke brought her another bouquet?

A dim gray light appeared a few feet behind her. Her vision was distorted both by the drug and by the black veil over her eyes. Still she thought she saw the outline of a woman in a full dress standing there. A pretty lady. A warm smile. How familiar she seemed. Was it the lady in the portrait? What portrait? She could not sort out her thoughts.

"Is that you, Moorduke?"

"No. I'm not your leprechaun, Ilene."

"Are you another fairy then?"

"No. But I am watching over you. You have been chosen."

"To be the bride of Satan?"

"There is no such thing as Satan, only the belief
229

in evil. He who poses as the warlock is as mortal as you are."

"Then what have I been chosen for?"

"*To become a Phenwick woman. To marry Gregory Phenwick.*"

"How do you know this?"

"*I know.*"

"Why am I being put through this terrible ordeal?"

"*It is the fate of those who become my successors. But I will be close at hand. Somehow I will help.*"

"Did you bring the scent of violets?"

"*I always bring it. It is the only way I have of making my presence known. Perhaps I'll find a different way in time. I will be close at hand. Each scene in life's drama must be played out for a reason. It is not always easy to comprehend, but there is a reason. I promise you will become a Phenwick woman.*" The vision slowly faded and the room was pitch dark again.

The apparition had not happened, Ilene told herself, it was only in her mind. Maybe all of her superstitious beliefs were all in her mind—including Moorduke.

The hazy cloud had lifted from her head, but her body was still itching with a kind of agony that could not be satisfied. Yet there moments when everything seemed perfectly clear and she would tell herself to endure the torment, that the drug would wear off.

The door opened and two deformed creatures in open robes entered. They did not speak but went directly to free her from the chair. With her hands still bound together, Ilene was taken across the hallway into that other room.

Black candles were lit and grotesque figures danced and cavorted in the flickering glow. They were parading about like insane people. Many appeared to be unclad or with their robes open.

As those who were holding her became amused by what was happening, Ilene felt their grip weaken. A hideous shadow leaped toward her. She pulled free and ran back toward the door. Before she could escape, Ilene was pounced on by the perverted people, literally lifted off the floor and carried about the room by the drunken communicants of the devil. She was pinched and grabbed, torn from one direction to another as gnarled hands seemed to blanket her with torment.

There was laughter, the kind one might hear when people have overimbibed liquor. Their dancing was lewd and vile words were flung at her.

Ilene's hands were untied and she was placed on the altar. Her feet were tied at each table leg, while her hands were put beneath the table and a rope wrapped around her chest and under the table to secure them. In the process she managed to grip a loop of rope in her hand unbeknown to her attackers.

Quivering with fear, but still somewhat hallucinating with the effect of the drug she had been given, Ilene stared hypnotically up at the inverted cross that was hanging directly above her. She kept telling herself it was all a dream, a dreadful nightmare, and it would soon pass.

Keeping her eyes on the cross, Ilene only caught glimpses of the diabolic celebration that was going on about her. She was convinced the people were completely mad, crazy.

A terrifying squawk penetrated the room, followed by the wild flapping sound of wings. She screamed in terror as a still flapping chicken was held above her, its blood splattering over her body. It was enough to make her regurgitate. The drug was already into her system and taking effect.

Ilene closed her eyes and cried out for Moorduke. The only reply was a faint aroma of violets. But she had become so panicked by then that she hardly recognized it. The spots of blood seemed to be burning through her gown as well as her skin. She screamed hysterically, turning her head from side to side as she did.

Her head was caught by two powerful hands.

At that moment a hush fell over the room. A gong was struck. Ilene could only barely see the image of the creature in the goathead mask and fleece jerkin. He danced about the room, going from one communicant to another as if seeking homage from each of them. The hands at her head moved her about so she could watch him.

The muffled sound of an incantation to the devil came from beneath the goathead mask. The others replied in recited verse. Louder and louder grew the incantation, commanding Satan himself to appear before them; and louder were the responses.

"The warlock approaches his bride!" a voice cried as the hands were removed from Ilene's face.

Ilene released the loop of rope she had been holding. It created enough slack that she could free her hands. Again the scent of violets. Somehow she took courage.

"So we came to this divine moment of ecstasy!"

the warlock stated, his voice still muffled. "The precious Ilene Dumphy has been placed upon the sacrificial altar. The moment of truth and revelation has arrived!"

"Don't touch me!" she screamed.

"I believe you have no choice, bride of Satan!" The voice was maniacal. "Where is your power to call forth an incubus now?" He laughed. "Once you have been desecrated, you will accept your position in the unholy kingdom. I have chosen you especially. You are to be honored above all the rest. It is my great act of magnitude! Do you understand?"

Ilene turned her head away from the hideous creature.

He put his hand to her hair, caressed it at first, then grabbed a firm hold. "Do you understand?"

"Moorduke!"

Leering eyes were watching. Lascivious giggles sprang from various parts of the room along with words of encouragement.

"Do you know who I am?" he asked, the masked face coming closer to hers.

She winced as he tightened his hold on her hair. At the same time she managed to pull the hand closest to the warlock free. Catching him off guard, she flung her hand upward and knocked the mask from his face.

She stared into the fierce eyes she knew only too well. "Yes, I know you, Gordon Phenwick"

A dreadful commotion sounded through the room as Gordon put a hand to his face to feel the mask was gone. Was he also drugged?

"I am a warlock! The supreme disciple of Satan! He works through me! My body is his!" Gordon shouted.

"But I can see your face, Reverend Phenwick. I know you," she said defiantly.

"Reverend? Reverend?" He called. "Do you hear what she calls me? My soul is black and I am the incarnation of Satan!"

"You're unmasked, Reverend Phenwick! Look in a mirror! The goathead is no longer hiding your identity," Ilene taunted.

"She speaks madness! Ah, but the more tempestuous the bride, the greater the delight." Gordon altered his position and his foot knocked against the mask. Slowly he loosened his hold and reached down to pick the goathead likeness up. "It is the face of Satan. It is my face. My *other* face!" With that, he quickly put the mask back in place. "The ceremony will continue! Do you hear me? The ceremony will continue!"

"You've become unmasked to these poor souls, too," Ilene stated. "They know now that you are merely another mortal like themselves."

"No! No! I'm not unmasked! I am Satan incarnate!" he yelled. "The ceremony will continue!"

Nobody moved as Gordon slowly turned about and scanned his followers.

CHAPTER TWENTY-FOUR

Sheila and Tim Dumphy had gone to Dr. Joseph's office. Only after they had made several inquiries were they given the address of his home.

Louise Ornby only knew that her son had had several evening calls to make on the sick. She did not know when to expect him home.

"There's only one thin' to it, Tim," Sheila stated. "We've got to go find that address on Elm Street."

"But I tell ya, I don't know th' precise number," her brother argued.

"You tol' me it was 1740 somethin', didn't ya?" Sheila questioned as she climbed into the cart.

"D'you know how bloomin' far it is to Elm Street?"

"Ten minutes if'n ya drive like ya know how."

"I can nay see what is so important about gittin' there so soon," Tim objected. "D'you want to spoil th' gent's fun?"

"Aye, d'you know what kind o' a man that Gordon Phenwick is?" Sheila shouted, taking the reins and starting the horse. "Dr. Joseph tol' me that he's sick in th' head, that's what he is."

"Sick?"

"There's nay tellin' what he might try t' do with Ilene," Sheila announced over the rumble of the

235

cart. "And if'n anythin' happens t' her, Timothy Dumphy, 'twill be you who's to blame."

Tim took the reins from his sister and pushed the horse as fast as he could toward Elm Street.

Joseph checked his watch as he reached his residence. Eight forty-five. If Myrtle Belcher was to be believed, he had to get to Elm Street immediately. His mother informed him that Sheila Dumphy and her brother had been there, saying that it concerned their sister, Ilene. That was all the verification Joseph needed. He got a fresh horse from the stable and rode in the saddle. His intention was to go to Edward House to get Stuart and Gregory. Recalling they were to be at Peter's for supper, he took a chance of catching them there. Besides, it was closer than the old house on Beacon Hill.

Arriving at Peter Phenwick's home, Joseph quickly dismounted, secured the horse and ran up to bang on the front door. He brushed past the butler when he learned that his cousins were still there.

"I'm sorry to burst in on everyone like this," Joseph apologized, "but I'm racing with the clock."

"What is it?" asked Stuart. "Can't you have a drink and catch your breath?"

"There's no time." Joseph exclaimed. "It's Gordon and I believe he has Ilene."

"Ilene?" Gregory was immediately to his feet.

"It's faster to go on horseback," Joseph said.

It was quickly decided that Gregory, Stuart, Jim Cornhill and Joseph would take horses to the Elm Street address. Peter would go for the authorities, accompanied by his son Thadius. That would take a while, and it would not be possible to get outside help to Elm Street before nine-thirty.

While the horses were being saddled, Joseph explained why he believed the matter was so urgent. "Gordon may well not realize that he has two different and distinct sides to his nature. First one takes over, then the other. I have observed him. However, I believe he is basically aware that he is a paradox, although I doubt we could ever get him to admit it. And I can't help but believe he justifies both sides of his nature by some quirk of rationality. I wish I knew more about this sort of thing. So little is known. And perhaps there are no two cases alike."

"What if we're too late?" Stuart questioned. "You don't suppose he might—I mean—he's not a killer."

"Let's hope he isn't," Joseph replied. He examined his watch. "We've got to hurry."

Gregory was seeing red. He leaped onto the horse and kicked it with a vengeance. He took the lead and remained in it until he had to lag back for directions. Then with Jim Cornhill bringing up the rear, the four went toward their destination, narrowly avoiding several mishaps with other vehicles en route.

In the 1000 block on Elm Street, the horsemen passed Tim and Sheila in the cart. Joseph simply waved back and motioned for them to follow.

Gordon had gone back to the throne. He realized he had to gather the support of the others, convince them that he really was the incarnation of Satan. But his followers had seen his face, were aware of the deception.

237

The congregation numbered twelve. Some were intoxicated enough that they were not disturbed by the unmasking, but others were obviously skeptical. As a result, he called forth the most trusted one and ordered that a special potion be mixed and passed among them.

"You are my people, the disciples of Satan!" he declared. "We have gathered here for the rites of Satan taking a bride, and we will see them to completion."

The profane host was passed among the cloaked figures. Many drank from it without reservation, while others were not certain they wanted to partake of the potent liquid. Gordon stomped around among them, administering to each and coercing those who were reluctant. When all had been served from the chalice, he drained the remaining contents.

"Now dance! And sing praise to Satan, our lord and master!" Gordon shrieked even as he felt himself reacting to the drink.

Ilene's eyes were ablaze with terror as she watched the spectacle. It was downright disgusting. Most of the time she stared straight above, only catching flickering shadows out of the corner of her eye.

When the dancing ceased and the communicants were fired into a frantic frenzy, Gordon raised his hands.

"It is nine-thirty! The moon is full!" he declared. "Satan will now be satisfied."

Ilene closed her eyes as she saw Gordon approaching. The terrible mask made him all the more sinister. Her body was still churning with that unnatural feeling, but her fear was so great that it surpassed all other sensation.

Gordon had put one knee on the altar and was about to lift himself onto it when he heard the sound. The stupefied followers whispered. One ran to the window and pulled the draperies back a crack. He motioned for Gordon.

Cautiously Gordon climbed down and crept toward the window, constantly aware of the faces that were watching him. Since it was difficult to see well through the mask, he appeared like a wary animal.

Slowly Gordon lifted the mask from his head and stared down into the street below. "Stuart," he muttered. "My brother." As he watched the four men mounting the steps, something happened within Gordon. His awareness snapped. Focusing on the mask in his hand, he suddenly flung it to the floor. A moment later he ripped the drapery from the wall and wrapped it around himself.

"Evildoers!" he roared. "Victims of your own lust and perverse natures! How dare you gather in this unholy place! Repent, for the day of salvation is at hand!"

The confused followers did not know how to react.

"Put a robe over that woman!" Gordon commanded. "And cover yourselves! I can only pray for your degenerate spirits!"

Gordon ran through the hall, the drapery slipping from him. He glanced back once at Ilene. In that moment the awful truth dawned on him. Tears came to his eyes as he made one last condemning statement and left the room.

Gordon took time only to put on his blouse and trousers. He carried his coat and shoes as he hurried down the back way.

The door had been broken through. Gordon could hear the men trying the inside doors on the first floor.

"I know Gordon owns this property," Stuart told Joseph. "I was here once. I told him he was a fool to purchase it."

"Upstairs!" Gregory yelled. "I hear someone up there!"

"There's a large room upstairs," Stuart commented, running behind his cousin.

Tim and Sheila arrived and followed the others. A spearlike object came flying through the air. Tim pushed his sister aside and caught the point of the weapon in his shoulder.

"'Tis nothin', Sheila," Tim exclaimed. "Go with th' others. But for God's sake be careful."

The hooded people came dashing from the ceremony room. They had chairs and whatever else they could find to use as weapons. The twisted bodies moved awkwardly, but they were no match for the strong young men.

Sheila pushed her way through the melee. One of the robes had been discarded. She took that to wrap about her sister.

"Are you all right, Ilene?" asked Sheila.

Ilene rolled her head from side to side. She could not speak. Tears had come to her eyes.

With effort, Sheila managed to free Ilene's hands and feet. Then she picked her up in her arms and cradled her like a small child. "Ah, me wee one, sure now, you had us worried. Are you able to talk to me, Ilene?"

"Yes. Hold me, Sheila, just hold me!" Ilene exclaimed.

"Aye, 'tis all right now. I have you in me arms."

"Reverend Phenwick—"

"We know it was Reverend Phenwick," Sheila said. " 'Twas Tim he paid to write that note to you askin' you to cum here. Th' men are roundin' them up now. Here, let me help you into this robe before th' men cum in."

"Mr. Phenwick?"

"Aye, there's at least two Mr. Phenwicks out there," Sheila replied.

"Gregory?"

"I don't know one from t'other. You'll just have to wait until they git that mess cleaned up."

Ilene broke into deep, uncontrolled crying.

Joseph entered. "Is she all right?"

"You had better have a look at her, Dr. Joseph," Sheila replied. "She's nay herself."

"I think they've got most of them," Joseph said as he went toward the altar. "Tim and Mr. Cornhill are holding them in a room downstairs."

"And Reverend Phenwick?" Sheila asked.

"The two Mr. Phenwicks are still searching for him," Joseph related. "This is a large house. He could be hiding anyplace. Now let me have a look at our girl." He examined her eyes. "Did they make you drink anything?"

"Something that was vile-tasting," Ilene said, her tongue thick and a terrible taste in her mouth.

"See if you can't find some water Sheila. We'll have to take her back to the office for a thorough going-over."

A short while later, after Sheila had discovered some water in a pitcher and had washed Ilene's face, Gregory and Stuart arrived.

"There's no sign of him anyplace," Stuart announced.

Gregory went straight to Ilene, nudged Joseph aside and took her in his arms. Unashamedly he kissed her in front of the others. As their lips met and she felt the security of his arms, Ilene passed out.

"What's wrong with her?" Gregory demanded.

"Goodness knows what she's been through this evening," Joseph returned. "We must get her to my office immediately. Sheila, you'll have to assist me."

"I'll help, too, Joseph," Gregory volunteered.

"What I'll have to do will not be pleasant to watch," the doctor returned. "You and Stuart had better see if you can find Gordon."

By then the authorities had arrived and they took charge of the prisoners. Although the cart was not the most comfortable vehicle, it was the only one available and Joseph felt an urgency to get Ilene under treatment. Jim Cornhill drove the cart, while Sheila rode in the back with Ilene. Joseph's horse kept time with the rumbling cart; then he urged it ahead to get the office prepared for the patient.

Twelve police officers, Peter, Thadius, Tim, Gregory and Stuart went over the old house from top to bottom. While they found many strange and suspicious articles, there was no sign whatsoever of Gordon.

"Unless there's some secret hiding place, we've lost him," the police lieutenant announced. "We'd better get these others back and see if we can't get to the bottom of all of this."

"Where do you suppose your brother could have gotten to, Stuart?" Gregory asked.

"I suggest we ride immediately to the church," Stuart stated, "then to his house. He's always been a strange person. There's no telling what's happened to him."

Later that night Gregory and Stuart arrived at Joseph's office to discover that Ilene seemed to be recovering.

"I suggest that Sheila and one of you boys stay here with Ilene through the night," Joseph said. "I don't think she should be moved before morning. What about Gordon?"

"There's no trace of him," Stuart replied, "although there is evidence that he departed from the church in a hurry—he carelessly left the office door open."

"You ought to have someone arrange to watch both his house and the church through the night," Joseph suggested.

"I'll take care of that," Stuart said.

Gregory went into the room where Ilene was sleeping. He glanced at Sheila, then gently placed a kiss on Ilene's brow. "I love her, Miss Dumphy—and I want her to be my wife."

CHAPTER TWENTY-FIVE

A thorough search was made for Gordon Phenwick over the next several days. He was not found. Speculation was made that he either was in hiding or had completely escaped the city—both of which were strong possibilities.

"Or like Judas Iscariot," Patricia had opined. "After betraying Christ, he went out and hanged himself. However, I don't believe Gordon capable of doing such a thing."

Stuart consulted with his cousin Daniel Ornby, the attorney. It was decided that Stuart, as closest relative, should have special locks put on all of Gordon's property—including the church.

A special investigation was set up by the authorities to look into all of Gordon's affairs. The list of unlawful things committed by the man grew to outrageous proportions. Stuart was embarrassed and did his best to keep the information from being circulated about. Daniel Ornby arranged financial settlements with persons who could have spread word of the preacher's scandalous affairs.

"I only pray," Stuart said, "that he has gone many miles from Boston, hopefully to the other side of the continent. Perhaps he will change his name."

"Did he take money with him?" asked Gregory.

"Cousin Daniel believes he got away with about fifty thousand dollars," Stuart replied. "Perhaps more. There is no telling exactly how much he had."

"What of his property here in Boston?"

"I'll manage it for a while. He has a business partner by the name of Angus Parson. Daniel is taking all the legal steps to put it in my control." Stuart sighed. "This has been very hard on all of us."

"Extremely difficult for Ilene," Gregory returned. "I say, she seems to have returned to her old self, but I know she has fear of Gordon. The poor girl will probably long have nightmares about the man until there is proof of his death."

"I have arranged to make a financial settlement to her from Gordon's property," Stuart said. "It is the least I can do."

"That's considerate, Stuart, but unnecessary," Gregory stated. "I've asked her to marry me. She has accepted. I want to take her back to England with me as soon as possible. She will feel safer out of Boston—and out of America, too."

"Are you acting in haste, Gregory?"

"In a sense I am," he replied, "but I am sincerely convinced of my love for her, and of hers for me. Her protection and best interest are foremost in my mind."

Stuart shook his cousin's hand in that fraternal way that was familiar to them. "I can only wish you the best of everything always. You have a beautiful person in Ilene."

While a more elaborate ceremony would be performed in London, a simple wedding ritual was arranged to take place in Patricia's chambers. Susannah and Jim would not be returning with the young couple, since Susannah feared her mother would not live much longer. Only the immediate family were to attend.

After the vows were exchanged, as the group felt it advisable not to remain too long with Patricia, they adjourned to the ballroom, where other guests had been invited for a reception.

Gregory kissed Patricia. "Grandmother—"

"I'm a very happy old lady today," Patricia said, clinging to the young man's hand. "My final project has been successfully completed. I am pleased."

"You'll find another project soon."

"I think not," Patricia sighed. "Come kiss me, Ilene. You're no longer a serving girl. You're now a Phenwick woman. And I give you both my blessing."

Ilene went to the bed and hugged the old lady as tightly as she dared. Her lips pressed the withered cheeks. "I will never forget you as long as I live, Mrs. Phenwick."

"It's Aunt Patricia now," the woman corrected. "The entire world will one day forget Patricia Kelburn Phenwick—as well they should. My poetry isn't much. I realize that now."

"You will always be as prominent as Augusta Phenwick in the eyes of the family," Gregory stated.

"What a ghastly thought!" exclaimed Patricia. "Still I promise not to haunt with the scent of violets. That's Augusta's department." She smiled dimly. "There's been so much excitement. I must have a nap—a prelude to a longer sleep. I love you both and wish you a beautiful life together all your days. It might be nice in the future, after this flesh is no longer usable, if there were to be another Patricia Phenwick. Not that I wish to influence you in the naming of your children, I was simply saying what might be nice."

"You can be certain that wish will be fulfilled, Grandmother," Gregory stated. He kissed her again. Then, taking his bride's hand, they left the old lady to nap as her new attendant sat quietly in the chair and watched her.

Sheila and Joseph Ornby had been at the wedding reception, but did not use the occasion to announce that they would be married when his father returned from Europe that fall.

On the day *The Patricia* embarked from Boston harbor, Sheila told Ilene of her plans to marry Dr. Joseph. Arrangements would be made to have an older woman come in and care for their father and the younger children. As Ilene kissed her sister goodbye, she was overcome with tears and it was a dramatic parting.

Tears still streamed down Ilene's face as she waved farewell. Gregory held tightly to her. Then, as the pier became only a spot in the distance, he took her in his arms and kissed her.

"Well, Ilene Phenwick," he said, "are you happy now?"

"I don't think I'll ever get used to being called Ilene Phenwick."

"You had better. I say, it would be terrible if you were addressed by some grand person and began gawking about to see to whom they were speaking," Gregory teased.

"Some grand person?" Ilene swallowed hard.

"Oh no, Gregory, I wouldn't know how to act around some grand person."

"Nonsense. You've acted yourself around one of the grandest persons in all the world while sitting with Grandmother," Gregory stated. "And my sister Marcia—and Mother. If they accept you as a Phenwick woman, then everyone else will. I love you, Ilene."

"And I love you, my darling," she replied.

"Shall we go below and see what the cabin is like? If it's not to your liking, I will have it changed especially for you."

"Would you really do that for me?"

"With all my heart and all my soul." He picked her up and carried her while the rough sailors observed with admiring looks.

On the evening of the third day out, Ilene already having adjusted to sea travel, Gregory asked if he might be excused for a while to confer with the captain on business matters. He would not be long. She might enjoy a stroll about the deck.

A warm shawl wrapped about her shoulders, Ilene climbed the steps to the deck. She had had little time to herself on the voyage, since Gregory managed to occupy most of her time. And she loved it. In London things would be different. He would have his work and his club. She would have to become acquainted with the notorious Joanna Phenwick, with Joshua and Olivia and their children. There would be many people to meet. A new way of life was opening up to her. She wondered if she would be capable of dealing with it. Of course she would.

The wind blew gently into her face, sweeping her hair back and flapping the shawl about her.

But she liked the sensation that came over her. An image of Gordon came to her mind, and she quickly forced it away as she had done whenever a thought of him or that dreadful night at 1743 Elm Street returned.

She stood defiantly at the prow, staring out into the vast sea. Was it all a dream from which she would soon awaken? Now she was convinced that the entire transformation of her life had been carefully and shrewdly arranged by Patricia Phenwick. She wondered if she would praise the old lady in time—or blame her for causing such a drastic change. She could only think it would be praise.

"You're a fine one, all uppity and high and mighty, ya are."

Ilene twirled around, believing someone had come up behind her. No one.

"Oh, I saw it cumin' frum th' day ya went into that fancy house."

"Moorduke?"

"Who else would be sneakin' up on ya like this? You're lookin' in th' wrong direction."

Ilene turned to see the small figure braced against a rope, hanging on for dear life. "Where have you been all this time?"

"Nearby. But I nay liked th' way what things were a-goin', so I did nay make meself seen to ya."

"You didn't like?"

"All them violets I was forced t' bring ya. It was a chore. And I'll tell ya th' truth, they made me sneeze."

"God bless you."

"Ya kin save that. I've stopped sneezin' now,

thank goodness. B'gorra, I'll be happy t' be back in Carrickfergus t' look up me auld mates."

"You were never happy in Boston, were you?"

"Nay after ya went t' that fancy Edward House. Aye, but when yer man cum along, then I knew it would niver be th' same agin. Mortals and fairies just aren't meant t' mix."

"I've always been very fond of you, Moorduke."

"Aye, as you were fond o' O'Ryan and other imaginary people you dreamed up. Well, I know me place, and you've found yers. I'm releasin' ya, Ilene. 'Tis folly t' think a leprechaun could keep a human bein' forever as his very own. Oooh, I know that now. But it took me a while t' learn."

"Moorduke—"

"Nay, hear me out. You see, I could nay ever compete with th' love yer man has for ya. That is somethin' else. Besides leprechauns don't fall in love anyway. Why, I'd be th' laughin'stock o' th' glen. As it is, me friends on th' heath will nay doubt point their fingers at me in scorn. I kin only be what I was meant t' be, just as you kin only be what you're meant t' be. B'gorra, it even takes us wee people time t' figure that out."

"I will always hold a special place for you in my thoughts, Moorduke."

"Aye, and that would be folly, too. You're best off t' forgit me. Now first I want t' congratulate ya on becomin' a Phenwick woman. I will nay say I did nay have me hand in that, for I did. Once I discovered yer man was frum England, I encouraged ya in me own way—by nay puttin' in an appearance. How else would I be able t' make this blasted trip across th' sea?"

"You encouraged? Because you wanted to go home?"

"Aye, 'tis true. And secondly I wish t' forgive ya for kickin' over me toadstool in th' fairy ring. I confess I was up t' mischief when I put it there. But even a fairy has t' have fun now and agin."

"I accept your apologies."

"You thought it was a mushroom all this time, but it was nay but a poison toadstool. I shall nay tell ya why I constructed such a mischievous ring in th' first place. 'Tis liable t' make ya blush."

"Why, Moorduke!"

" 'Tis true. A leprechaun has passions, too. Now, I will say farewell t' you, lass."

"Farewell?"

"You will niver see th' likes o' me agin. I have a lot o' rompin' t' catch up with in th' glen. And you've nay longer need o' me. I'll stay aboard for th' ride, but you won't know where I am. 'Tis best, lass. Once I git to England, 'twill only be a hop, skip and a jump to find me way back t' Ireland and Carrickfergus. It has ben a pleasant little friendship we've had. And maybe one day you'll tell yer children about me—but do so in jest—you wouldn't want 'em t' think ya was balmy, would ya? Little Patricia, I mean, and th' rest. Goodbye, Ilene."

The tiny figure changed into a glow of light and then completely disappeared.

Tears had come to Ilene's eyes. "Moorduke! Wait, Moorduke! You forgot to let me say—goodbye."

Two strong hands were firmly clasped about Ilene's waist. Warm lips pressed to the back of her neck as the hands gently caressed her body.

"Talking to yourself, my darling?" asked Gregory as he turned her about to kiss him.

"No—I mean—" His mouth was covering hers.

"No?" Gregory asked several moments later.

"I mean—" She glanced to the rope where she had seen the last fading glow. "Yes, I suppose I was speaking to myself. There is a time when we put fantasies and superstitions away, isn't there?"

"If there isn't, I say, there should be."

Gregory kissed her again and warmly held her in his arms.

A while later she stood with her back to him as they both faced the horizon of their new tomorrow. Ilene looked down to the rope. For a moment she thought she beheld a tiny bouquet of violets— but only for a moment. She turned her head back to kiss her husband again as a proper Phenwick woman should.

CAST OF CHARACTERS

Sean Dumphy   An Irish emigrant who settled in Boston with his wife and ten children.

Mary Dumphy   His wife.

Sheila Dumphy   The eldest daughter.

Tim Dumphy   The eldest son, just younger than Sheila.

Ilene Dumphy   The pretty third Dumphy daughter, fifth child in the family. Imaginative and superstitious, she is a delightful puzzle to all who know her.

Moorduke   Ilene's friend?

Stella Murphy   Another Irish emigrant who is hired to attend to Patricia Phenwick in declining years.

Angus Parson   Gordon Phenwick's business adviser.

Myrtle Belcher   An old crone with very curious beliefs.

Joseph Ornby   Son of Dr. Theodore Ornby and cousin to the reigning Phenwicks of Boston. He, like his father, is a physician.

Dietrich   The butler at Edward House.

Nora

Mattie   Servants at Edward House.

THE PHENWICKS

—AUGUSTA — Founder of the family. She maintains an eerie hold over the surviving members.

—DANIEL — Augusta's only son who lived to adulthood. Father of Elias (by Kate Mumford); married to Margaret O'Plaggerty, and father of Alexander, Peter and Rachel.

—ELIAS — Married to Patricia Kelburn; father of Rebecca.

—REBECCA — Only daughter of Elias and Patricia, first married to Johnny Ornby, becoming foster-mother to Adrianne and Lydia; second marriage to Robert Cathcart, mother of Kate Phenwick.

—KATE PHENWICK — Daughter of Rebecca and granddaughter of Patricia. She is a young beauty disturbed by the sensation that the houses of the Phenwick family haunt her with distant memories.

—ALEXANDER — Married to Susannah Phenwick and adopted father of Marcia and Gregory.

—MARCIA — An English peasant girl adopted with her brother into the Phenwick family.

—GREGORY — Handsome brother of Marcia. Resides in England.